致敬译界巨匠许渊冲先生

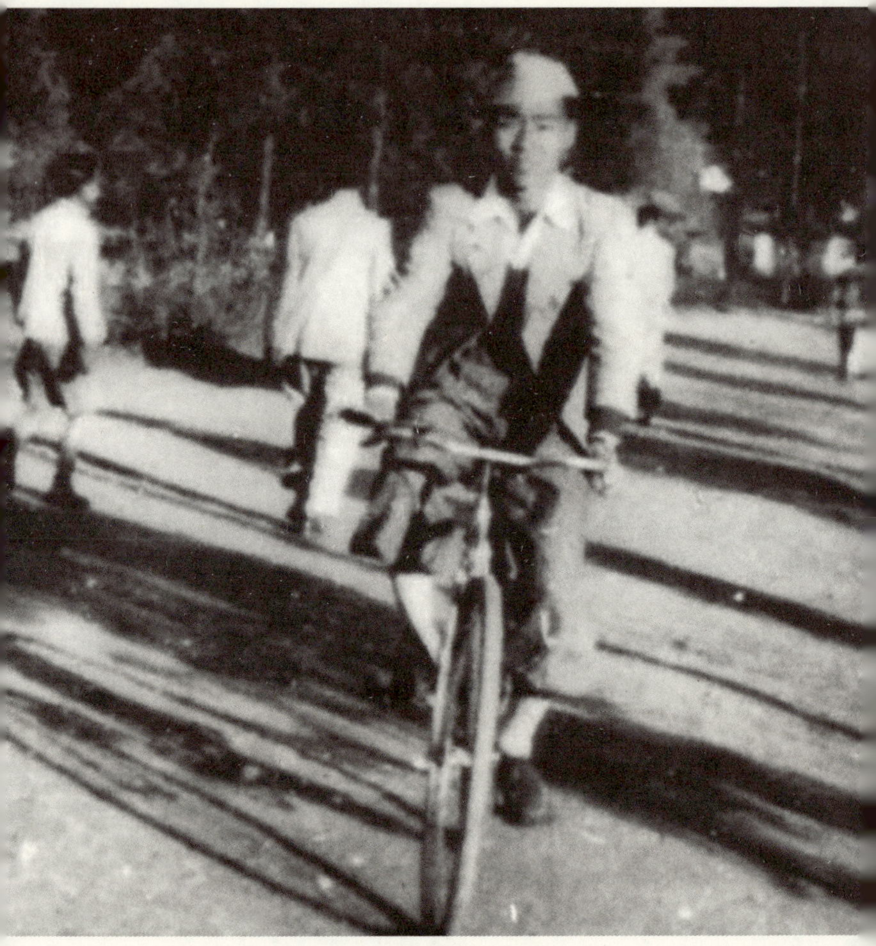

许 渊 冲 译
李 白 诗 选

SELECTED POEMS OF LI BAI

| 编 | 译 |

中国出版集团
中译出版社

目录 Contents

| 译序
Translator's Preface

002 访戴天山道士不遇
Calling on a Taoist Recluse in Daitian Mountain without Meeting Him

004 登锦城散花楼
On the Flowery Tower in the Town of Silk

006 峨眉山月歌
The Moon over the Eyebrow Mountains

008 巴女词
Song of a Woman of Ba

010 荆州歌
The Silk Spinner

012 渡荆门送别
Farewell Beyond the Thorn-Gate Gorge

014 望庐山瀑布水（二首其二）
The Waterfall in Mount Lu Viewed from Afar (II)

016 望庐山五老峰
The Five Greybeard-like Peaks of Mount Lu Viewed from Afar

018 望天门山
Mount Heaven's Gate Viewed from Afar

020 杨叛儿
A Love Song

022 长干行（二首其一）
Ballads of a Merchant's Wife (I)

026 长干行（二首其二）
Ballads of a Merchant's Wife (II)

030 金陵酒肆留别
Parting at a Tavern in Jinling

032 夜下征虏亭
　　 Passing by the Triumphal Tower at Night

034 上李邕
　　 The Roc—to Li Yong

036 静夜思
　　 Thoughts on a Silent Night

038 黄鹤楼送孟浩然之广陵
　　 Seeing Meng Haoran off at Yellow Crane Tower

040 长相思（二首其一）
　　 Lovesickness (I)

042 长相思（二首其二）
　　 Lovesickness (II)

044 登新平楼
　　 Ascending Xinping Tower

046 蜀道难
　　 Hard Is the Road to Shu

052 行路难（三首其一）
　　 Hard Is the Way of the World (I)

056 行路难（三首其二）
　　 Hard Is the Way of the World (II)

060 行路难（三首其三）
　　 Hard Is the Way of the World (III)

064 送友人入蜀
　　 To a Friend Departing for Shu

066 春夜洛城闻笛
　　 Hearing a Bamboo Flute on a Spring Night in Luoyang

068 塞下曲（六首其一）
　　 Frontier Song (I)

070 关山月
　　 The Moon over the Mountain Pass

072 乌夜啼
The Crows Crying at Night

074 春思
A Faithful Wife Longing for Her Husband in Spring

076 三五七言
Yearning

078 怨情
Waiting in Vain

080 玉阶怨
Waiting in Vain on Marble Steps

082 长门怨（二首其一）
Sorrow of the Long Gate Palace (I)

084 长门怨（二首其二）
Sorrow of the Long Gate Palace (II)

086 子夜吴歌（春歌）
Ballads of Four Seasons (Spring)

088 子夜吴歌（夏歌）
Ballads of Four Seasons (Summer)

090 子夜吴歌（秋歌）
Ballads of Four Seasons (Autumn)

092 子夜吴歌（冬歌）
Ballads of Four Seasons (Winter)

094 将进酒
Invitation to Wine

098 赠孟浩然
To Meng Haoran

100 夜泊牛渚怀古
Thoughts on Old Time from a Night-Mooring near Cattle Hill

102 客中行
While Journeying

104 陌上赠美人
To a Fair Lady Encountered on the Road

106 登太白峰
Ascending the Snow-White Peak

108 登广武古战场怀古
Reflections on the Ancient Battlefield at Guangwu

112 南陵别儿童入京
Parting from My Children at Nanling for the Capital

114 清平调词（三首其一）
The Beautiful Lady Yang (I)

116 清平调词（三首其二）
The Beautiful Lady Yang (II)

118 清平调词（三首其三）
The Beautiful Lady Yang (III)

120 忆东山（二首其一）
The Eastern Hill (I)

122 乌栖曲
Crows Going Back to Their Nest—Satire on the King of Wu

124 下终南山过斛斯山人宿置酒
Descending Zhongnan Mountain and Meeting Husi the Hermit

126 月下独酌（四首其一）
Drinking Alone under the Moon (I)

128 把酒问月
Reflections on the Moon While Drinking

132 白云歌送刘十六归山
Song of White Cloud—Farewell Song to Liu the Recluse

134 秋日鲁郡尧祠亭上宴别杜补阙范侍御
Farewell to Two Friends in Lu on an Autumn Day

136 鲁郡东石门送杜二甫
Farewell to Du Fu at Stone Gate

138 沙丘城下寄杜甫
To Du Fu from Sand Hill Town

140 戏赠杜甫
Addressed Humorously to Du Fu

142 梦游天姥吟留别
Mount Skyland Ascended in a Dream—A Song of Farewell

150 登金陵凤凰台
On Phoenix Terrace at Jinling

152 劳劳亭
Pavilion Laolao

154 丁都护歌
Song of the Tow-men

156 苏台览古
The Ruin of the Gusu Palace

158 越中览古
The Ruin of the Capital of Yue

160 越女词 （五首其一）
Songs of the Southern Lass (I)

162 越女词（五首其三）
Songs of the Southern Lass (III)

164 越女词（五首其五）
Songs of the Southern Lass (V)

166 渌水曲
Song of Green Water

168 闻王昌龄左迁龙标遥有此寄
To Wang Changling Banished to the West

170 战城南
Fighting South of the Town

174 听蜀僧濬弹琴
On Hearing a Monk from Shu Playing His Lute

176	寄东鲁二稚子	
	Written for My Two Children in East Lu	
180	秦王扫六合	
	The Emperor of Qin	
184	登高丘而望远海	
	Mounting a Height and Viewing the Sea	
188	北风行	
	The North Wind	
192	横江词（六首其一）	
	The Crosswise River (I)	
194	山中问答	
	A Dialogue in the Mountain	
196	自遣	
	Solitude	
198	独坐敬亭山	
	Sitting Alone in Face of Peak Jingting	
200	宣州谢朓楼饯别校书叔云	
	Farewell to Uncle Yun, the Imperial Librarian, at Xie Tiao's Pavilion in Xuanzhou	
204	秋登宣城谢朓北楼	
	On Ascending the North Tower One Autumn Day	
206	送友人	
	Farewell to a Friend	
208	秋浦歌（十七首其十四）	
	Songs of Autumn Pool (XIV)	
210	秋浦歌（十七首其十五）	
	Songs of Autumn Pool (XV)	
212	赠汪伦	
	To Wang Lun Who Comes to Bid Me Farewell	
214	哭晁卿衡	
	Elegy on Abe Nakamaro	

216 永王东巡歌（十一首其二）
Song of Eastern Expedition of Prince Yong (II)

218 与史郎中钦听黄鹤楼上吹笛
On Hearing the Flute in Yellow Crane Tower

220 早发白帝城
Leaving the White Emperor Town for Jiangling

222 与夏十二登岳阳楼
Ascending the Tower of Yueyang with Xia the Twelfth

224 陪族叔刑部侍郎晔及中书贾舍人至游洞庭（五首其二）
On Lake Dongting (II)

226 江上吟
Song on the River

228 夜宿山寺
The Summit Temple

230 庐山谣寄卢侍御虚舟
Song of Mount Lu — To Censor Lu Xuzhou

234 豫章行
Song of Yuzhang

238 哭宣城善酿纪叟
Elegy on Master Brewer Ji of Xuancheng

240 宣城见杜鹃花
Azalea Blooms Viewed in Xuancheng

242 临终歌
On Death-Bed

译序

（一）

李白是我国唐代最伟大的浪漫主义诗人。浪漫主义作为一种文艺思潮，是欧洲18世纪末至19世纪初的社会产物，但是作为创作方法却像现实主义一样，是和文学艺术同时产生的。现实主义更侧重客观事物的描绘，浪漫主义更侧重主观感情的抒发。用中国诗艺的术语"比兴赋"来描述，现实主义作品多用赋的方法，浪漫主义多用比兴的方法。而运用比兴正是李白诗歌的一大特点。

李白生于公元701年，故乡是今天四川江油县的青莲乡。他的少年时代正当唐玄宗"开元之治"前期，那时玄宗励精图治，整个社会欣欣向荣。李白从少年时代起就胸怀大志，想把自己的文才武艺都奉献给大唐王朝，想做布衣卿相，以使国泰民安。公元725年，李白25岁，经由长江三峡出蜀，一路写了《峨眉山月歌》《渡荆门送别》等诗。到金陵后，又写了《长干行》《金陵酒肆留别》等。五年后，他第一次到唐代的京城长安，发现有志难酬，心中苦闷，于是写了《长相思》《行路难》《蜀道难》等。这一批诗歌在李白一生的创作中形成了第一个高潮，反映了他第一次到长安的遭遇和思想感情。作品有些是直抒胸臆，有些是

I

比兴言志，而《蜀道难》是以行路艰难比喻仕途坎坷，感慨报国无门的一篇杰作。

李白离开长安之后，沿着黄河南下。公元735年，与友人在嵩山南麓置酒高会，写下了《将进酒》一诗，感慨盛年易逝，功业未立，但仍寄希望于未来。直到公元742年秋天，他已名满天下，方才奉诏入京。这时唐玄宗已经成了一个"春宵苦短日高起，从此君王不早朝"的安乐天子。他召李白进京，并不是为了任用贤才治理国家，只是需要一个出色的文人侍候他吃喝玩乐，点缀太平岁月，所以李白这时的名作是为杨贵妃写的《清平调》。杜甫写的《饮中八仙歌》写出了他在长安的生活。李白自知不为朝廷重用，三年后上书请求"还山"。玄宗也认为他不是治国之才，就赐金放他回乡。

公元746年，李白有越中之行，行前写了《梦游天姥吟留别》。这首诗和《蜀道难》一样，也是用比兴手法挥斥幽愤，借梦游仙山写他第二次到长安"攀龙堕天"的经历，所以最后两句说："安能摧眉折腰事权贵，使我不得开心颜！"公元753年，李白在宣城与族叔李华登谢朓楼，写了一首《登楼歌》，也是愤世的作品。公元755年，安禄山造反，永王出兵讨伐，聘请李白入幕，不料永王和太子的矛盾演变为内战。永王败死，李白也被判处流放夜郎。公元759年春，李白到白帝城，遇赦获释，返回江陵，写下了著名的《早发白帝城》。公元760年，李白年已六十，再登庐山，又写了《庐山谣寄卢侍御虚舟》一诗，借用楚狂人嘲笑孔子的故事，暗示朝廷昏暗，从政危险，不如修仙学道。第二年他重游宣城，写了两首同情人民的诗：《宿五松山下荀媪家》和《哭宣城善酿纪叟》。公元762年，李白死于当涂，据说是醉后入水捉月而死。

纵观李白一生，从青年时代起，直到逝世之前，都在为实现济苍生、安社稷的理想而奋斗。因为他身上浸透了伟大的政治理想和报国热情,发而为诗,自然充满了浓郁的时代气息,代表了广大人民的思想感情。他一生的经历,同盛唐时期的国运,几乎是息息相关的。早期的生活似乎充满了阳光,诗作也呈现出一派天朗气清、风和日丽的景象。诗中很少感慨,更无牢骚,即使是抒写离情别绪,也使人心旷神怡。开元中期,唐玄宗封泰山之后,骄侈之心日长,图治之心日消,李白诗中便也呈现出明暗交错、悲欢杂糅的特点。到了李白晚年,安史之乱后期,诗中又曾出现过希望的闪光,结果还是幻影破灭。于是他又立心修仙学道,浪迹江湖,这时即使寻欢作乐,也不过是强颜为欢,甚至是狂歌当哭了。

陈毅同志说过:"吾读李白诗,喜有浪漫味。大不满现实,遂为游仙醉。"可见李白的山水诗、神仙诗、饮酒诗、爱情诗,实际上大都是政治抒情诗,含有现实内容。因此可以说,李白是我国古代最伟大的浪漫主义诗人。现在把他的诗译成具有意美、音美、形美的英文,我希望能和全世界的英语读者共享中国古诗之美。

(二)

李白是代表盛唐文化的诗人。我国古代黄河流域的北方文化,在哲学思想方面,以孔子的《论语》为代表,在文学艺术方面,以现实主义的《诗经》为典型。长江流域的南方文化在哲学上的代表是老子《道德经》,在文学上的典型是浪漫主义的《离骚》。而李白却是南北文化融合的典型代表。他的生平可以用杜甫的《赠李白》来概括:

秋来相顾尚飘蓬,未就丹砂愧葛洪。
痛饮狂歌空度日,飞扬跋扈为谁雄?

李白到了生命的秋天,还不能实现儒家入世的理想,为国为民,尽心竭力,而只能像一片浮云,一团飘蓬,只身漂流四方。他也不能实现道家出世的理想,求仙学道,炼丹升天,求得精神上的自由解脱。他只能高歌吟诗,狂饮度日,来浇愁解闷,正如杜甫在《饮中八仙歌》说的:

李白一斗诗百篇,长安市上酒家眠。
天子呼来不上船,自称臣是酒中仙。

这就是一个天才的悲剧,他像一个从天上贬到人间的"谪仙",英雄无用武之地。什么时候他才能实现凌霄壮志,像庄子说的大鹏鸟那样"抟扶摇而上者九万里"呢?

李白的诗有雄浑的一面,也有飘逸的一面。雄浑的如《望庐山瀑布水》:

日照香炉生紫烟,遥看瀑布挂前川。
飞流直下三千尺,疑是银河落九天。

这首诗是李白26岁第一次游庐山时的作品。巍巍的香炉峰上白云缭绕,在红日照耀下形成一片紫雾,仿佛冉冉上升的云烟,要把庐山和青天融成一片。瀑布像一条巨大的白练高挂在山川之间,在青山的衬托之下,云烟也似乎成了四溅的水珠,喷涌而下,简直就像银河从天而降,这样又把青天和庐山融成一片。气势雄浑,大有开天辟地之感。一个"生"

字，一个"挂"字，把山水都拟人化了，大有神工鬼斧之妙。如果不是神仙，谁能把瀑布高挂在庐山之上呢？这样，银河自上而下，云烟自下而上，就把天地融成混沌一片了。至于李白诗的飘逸风格，可以读他的《山中问答》：

问余何意栖碧山，笑而不答心自闲。
桃花流水窅然去，别有天地非人间。

这首绝句读来飘飘欲仙，超凡脱俗，有问无答。第一句问；第二句自叙面笑心闲，说明诗人热爱自由；第三句描写碧山之美，说明诗人热爱自然；第四句作结，说明山中别有天地，可算人间天堂。从诗中可以看出李白对美的热爱，以及遗世独立的风格。

李白写诗，爱用比兴手法，而比兴所用的形象，有的洋溢着阳刚的豪气，有的流露出柔和的秀气。有豪气的形象如大鹏鸟，在《上李邕》中，李白写道：

大鹏一日同风起，扶摇直上九万里。
假令风歇时下来，犹能簸却沧溟水。

大鹏其翼如垂天之云，可以凌霄冲天，正好象征诗人的凌云壮志。即使风停云散，也能掀起万丈波涛。可见气势之大，余波之威。乘风破浪，都可象征诗人对自由的热爱。流露出灵秀之气的形象如明月，最著名的例子是《静夜思》：

床前明月光，疑是地上霜。
举头望明月，低头思故乡。

明月是圆的，所以中国人看见明月，就会想到一家人团圆。但是西方人并没有团圆的观念，所以看到明月不一定会想到家庭团聚，同一个形象引起的联想并不相同，这是文化背景的关系。所以译成英文的时候，只好把第一句的"明月光"说成"一池月光"。又把第四句的"思故乡"说成是"沉浸在乡愁中"，这样就把月光和乡愁都比作水，二者之间才有联系。这就是说，中文用"圆"的形象联系起来的明月和思乡，在英文中改用水的形象联系起来了，由此也可看出诗人对自然的热爱。总之，文化交流，应该以互相沟通为目的，方法可以根据目的而改变。

译者把月光和乡愁都比作水，并不是译者凭空虚构，而是根据李白所用的比兴手法演绎出来的。李白在描写自然风景时，想象力丰富，如《梦游天姥吟留别》中说：

> 列缺霹雳，丘峦崩摧。

但在描写人的抽象情感时，反而用具体的自然风景来做比较。如下面三个例子：

> 请君试问东流水，别意与之谁短长？（《金陵酒肆留别》）
> 浮云游子意，落日故人情。（《送友人》）
> 桃花潭水深千尺，不及汪伦送我情。（《赠汪伦》）

第一例把别意比作流水，可见情意长远；第二例把不可见的离情比成可见的浮云落日，形象生动；第三例把友情比作湖水，可见情深。三个例子都把情感比成自然景物。在翻译时,把可见的月光和不可见的乡愁都比作水,应该是符合李白风格的。译者应该假设:如果李白是今天的英美诗人,他写《静夜思》会如何遣词造句呢?这时译者就要先化身成李白,再用英文来表达诗情词义了,从这个意义上来说,译诗是再创作。

从以上的送别诗中,可以看出李白多么重视友情。而在抒发友情的送别诗中,最著名的一首可能是《黄鹤楼送孟浩然之广陵》:

故人西辞黄鹤楼,烟花三月下扬州。
孤帆远影碧空尽,惟见长江天际流。

这首七绝作于公元728年,那时李白二十七八岁,孟浩然却已四十了。李白写过一首《赠孟浩然》,诗中说道:"吾爱孟夫子,风流天下闻。红颜弃轩冕,白首卧松云。"从中可以看出他对孟浩然的敬仰。他们分别的地方是黄鹤楼,就是仙人乘鹤登天的地方,因此看到友人离别,也会想到仙人升天;看到白帆远去,又会想到黄鹤高飞。这样,诗一开始就笼罩在一片灵光仙气之中,天地似乎融成一片,人也似乎和天地合一了。其次,孟浩然要去的广陵,就是今天的扬州,当时是全国,甚至可以说是全世界最繁华的都市,而他们分别的时间又是杨柳如烟、繁花似锦的阳春三月,可以说是在最好的时光去到最好的地方,因此这句诗被誉为"千古丽句"。从黄鹤楼到广陵,长江两岸都花红柳绿,沉浸在一片美丽而幸福的氛围中。李白站在楼前,望着友人的帆船渐行渐远,消失在青天白云之间,仿佛像黄鹤一样融入了万里长空。这里我们可以想象诗人的心灵也融入天际了。最后,诗人眼里看到的只是不尽长江滚滚来，我们可以感到诗人心潮澎湃，犹如汹涌的波涛，越流越远，无穷无尽。这既象征了诗人对友人的思念，也暗示了诗人自己的凌霄壮志，冲涛破浪，一往无前。这首短诗前两句叙事，后两句写景，没有一句抒情的话，但是句句景语都是情语。从描写的景色中，我们可以感到诗人对友人的深情厚谊。这种借景写情的手法，是李白诗的一个特点，也是我国诗词和西方诗不同的地方。

不只是友情诗，就是男女之间的爱情诗也是一样。西方诗人，尤其是英国浪漫主义诗人，无论谈情说爱，都是直叙胸臆，直截了当，掏心沥血，倾诉衷肠。唐宋诗人却不相同，多是含蓄不露，借景写情，以巧制胜，以少胜多。例如李白的《春思》：

燕草如碧丝，秦桑低绿枝。
当君怀归日，是妾断肠时。
春风不相识，何事入罗帏？

诗题中的"春"字，既可以指自然界的春天，又可以托喻男女之间的爱情。第一句的"丝"字，既可以指丝线，也可以谐音指"相思"。就是说在北方的妻子，看见萋萋芳草绿了，自然会想起在西方的夫君怎么还不回家，是不是桑叶太多，压弯了树枝呢？而"枝"字又可谐音"知"，就是说夫君是不是忙于丝绸的生意，因蚕桑而不"知"回家呢？由此可以看出古诗转弯抹角，一点也不直截了当，而是含蓄不露。燕草和秦桑则是借景写情。第三、四句还是想象，不是事实，夫君不归，妻子相思得要断肠了，可见爱情之深。最后两句更是特写，说春风吹开了妻子床上的帐子，妻子却怪春风不尊重她的隐私，擅自闯入卧房。连春风都不许进来，更不用说陌生人了，由此可以看出妻子对夫君的忠贞爱情，也可看出李白构思的巧妙。一个例子就能举一反三，可以算是以少胜多了。

李白的诗，无论是写友情或是爱情，都不带有悲观色彩。即使是写悲情，他也不太会用痛苦绝望的字眼。总的说来，他的诗显得平静乐观，这种乐观精神似乎出自他对生命和艺术的信念，出自他对精神自由与天人合一的不断追求。他的追求精神表现在《行路难》中，如：

长风破浪会有时，直挂云帆济沧海。

如果他感到失意或悲哀，就会买酒痛饮，借酒浇愁，如他在《将进酒》中说：

五花马，千金裘，呼儿将出换美酒，与尔同销万古愁！

既然说"万古愁"，那就不是个人的痛苦，而是千年万代，人所共有的愁恨了。他对天人合一的追求，可以从《独坐敬亭山》中看出：

众鸟高飞尽，孤云独去闲。
相看两不厌，只有敬亭山。

"孤云独去闲"中的"孤"和"闲"，不但是说天上的云，也是指地上的人，诗人和天上的云一样孤独、一样悠闲，这就是天人合一了。"相看两不厌"是说：人看山看不厌，山看人也看不厌，这也是达到了山人合一的境界，都说明了诗人对自然或对天的热爱。还有一个例子是《早发白帝城》：

> 朝辞白帝彩云间，千里江陵一日还。
> 两岸猿声啼不住，轻舟已过万重山。

白帝城在彩云之间，这似乎是仙居；一日可行千里，这在唐代可算神速；猿鹤都是仙侣，能过万重山的轻舟自然是天河中的仙槎。第一句写空间，第二句写时间，第三句写动物，第四句写静物。无论时空动静，诗人都和神仙合而为一。无怪乎李白被称为"谪仙"了。

李白不但热爱自由和自然，也热爱美人，如《越女词》第五首：

> 镜湖水如月，耶溪女如雪。
> 新妆荡新波，光景两奇绝。

"女如雪"把美人和自然美结合起来，这也是一种天人合一吧。不过李白继承屈原用香草和美人来象征君王的传统，有时字面上看起来是说美人，实际上却是指君王，如在《长相思》中说：

> 长相思，在长安……美人如花隔云端。

李白在长安并没有情人，即使有也不可能"隔云端"，所以美人是指皇帝。天高皇帝远，李白不受重用，政治抱负不能实现，所以就借美人抒怀了。李白对皇帝的不满，还表

现在他的讽刺诗中,如他在《古风》(其三)中讽刺秦始皇派徐福去海上寻求长生不老之药,结果还是:

但见三泉下,金棺葬寒灰!

至于他对劳动人民的同情,则体现在《丁都护歌》等诗中,这里就不一一列举了。

(三)

李白是我国在国外最著名的古代诗人。他的第一个英译本是1922年由小畑薰良翻译,由纽约达顿公司出版的,闻一多教授在1926年写了一篇评论文章。第二个英译本包括在威利的《李白的生平和诗歌》一书中,由英国阿伦及安文公司于1950年出版。第三个英译本包括在库柏翻译的《李白和杜甫》一书中,由英国企鹅图书公司于1973年出版。至于英美出版的《中国古代诗选》,选用李白的诗很多,这里不能一一列举。自1980年起,《李白诗选》的英译本多由国内出版。据范存忠教授在《外国语》中说:李白对英国浪漫主义诗人有过影响。这个问题我没有进行过研究,不过可以做个简单的比较。英国诗人可以用他们喜爱的飞鸟来代表:如华兹华斯的杜鹃、柯尔律治的信天翁、拜伦的雄鹰、雪莱的云雀、济慈的夜莺。那么,李白的象征就是大鹏鸟了。《上李邕》中说:"大鹏一日同风起,扶摇直上九万里。假令风歇时下来,犹能簸却沧溟水。"如果说美国意象派诗人庞德和洛威尔翻译的李白诗是"沧溟水"的话,那这个新译本就要"扶摇直上九万里"了。

Translator's Preface

(I)

Li Bai (701–762) is regarded as the greatest romantic poet of the Tang Dynasty (618–907) and of China of all times. Romanticism, according to Macmillan English Dictionary, is a style of literature, art, and music common at the end of the 18th and beginning of the 19th centuries that emphasized the importance of personal feelings and of nature. But as a method of writing, romanticism and realism co-exist with art and literature: romanticism is more subjective while realism is more objective. To use three terms in Chinese poetics, we may say "narration" (or "description") is often used in realistic works while "comparison" and "association" (or similes and metaphors) are used in romantic works. In Li Bai's poetry, we may find many similes and metaphors.

Born in 701 at the Lotus Village of Riverside County (in modern Sichuan Province), Li Bai passed his youth during the reign of Emperor Xuan Zong (or Bright Emperor 713–741) when the Tang Dynasty enjoyed its highest prosperity, so the young poet cherished a lofty aspiration to serve the country with might and main. In 725, Li Bai left his homeland at the age of twenty-five, passed the Three Gorges and travelled along the Yangtze River, when he wrote *The Moon over the Eyebrow Mountains* and *Farewell beyond the Thorn-Gate Gorge*, in which both the moon and water are personified, and which reveal his deep love of nature as well as of his native land. Arrived at Jinling, he wrote *Ballads of a Merchant's Wife* and *Parting at a Tavern in Jinling*. Five years later he came for the first time to Chang'an, the Tang capital, in the hope of meeting people of influence who might help him to realize his political ideal. Disappointed, he wrote *Lovesickness* in which he compared his yearning to the love for a woman, *Hard Is the Way of the World* and *Hard Is the Road to Shu* which is supposed to be his most important work in the first period of his verse-making.

In 735, he wrote *Invitation to Wine* in which he revealed his love of drink was due to his disappointment in his career. Famed for his poetry, he was summoned to the capital in 742 to write poems and songs for the emperor and his favorite mistress, of which the best-known are the three stanzas on *The Beautiful Lady Yang*. In 744 he left Chang'an for Luoyang where he met Du Fu and a warm friendship and exchange of poems began and lasted lifelong. In 746, he travelled in the south and wrote *Mount Skyland Ascended in a Dream* which ends in the following verse:

> *How can I stoop and bow before the men in power*
> *And so deny myself a happy hour?*

In 753, he visited Xuancheng (in modern Anhui Province) and wrote many poems in the pavilion of Xie Tiao, including the following lines:

Cut running water with a sword, 'twill faster flow;
Drink wine to drown your sorrow, it will heavier grow.

In 755, An Lushan raised the standard of rebellion, and Li Bai was called to join the loyal forces led by Prince Yong in an attempt to resist the rebels. His political aspirations revived and he wrote his *Song of Eastern Expedition of Prince Yong*. When the Prince was defeated, he was banished to Yelang (in modern Guizhou Province) until an amnesty was declared in 759. When he regained his liberty, he wrote his joyful quatrain *Leaving the White Emperor Town for Jiangling* (others believe it was written much earlier). In 760, he revisited the Lu Mountains (in modern Jiangxi Province) and wrote the *Song of Mount Lu*, which manifests his conversion to Taoism. In 762, he died at the age of sixty-two, chanting his last verse *On Death-Bed*.

(II)

Li Bai is representative of High Tang culture, the combination of Northern culture represented by Confucian philosophy and the *Book of Poetry*, and the Southern culture represented by Taoist philosophy and the *Elegies of the South*. His life may be summed up by Du Fu's quatrain *To Li Bai*:

When autumn comes, you're drifting still like thistledown;
You try to find the way to Heaven, but you fail.
In singing mad and drinking dead your days you drown.
O when will fly the roc, and when will leap the whale?

In the autumn of his life, Li Bai could not fulfil his Confucian ideal to serve the country but wander lonely like a drifting cloud. Nor could he find spiritual freedom in Taoism, which taught him to seek the way to Heaven. So he could not but chant poetry and drink wine to drown his sorrow as described by Du Fu in *Eight Immortal Drinkers*:

Li Bai could turn sweet nectar into verses fine;
Drunk in the capital, he'd lie in shops of wine.
Even imperial summons proudly he'd decline,
Saying immortals could not leave the drink divine.

Here we see the tragedy of a genius staying lonely on earth like an angel fallen from Heaven. When could he realize his aspiration to fly to the sky like the fabulous roc?

Li Bai's poetry is marked by masculine grandeur and natural grace. For instance, *The Waterfall in Mount Lu Viewed from Afar* is typical of its grandeur:

The sunlit Censer Peak exhales incense-like cloud;
The cataract hangs like upended stream sounding loud.
Its torrent dashes down three thousand feet from high

As if the Silver River fell from azure sky.

He wrote this quatrain probably at twenty-six when he first visited the Lu Mountains in northern Jiangxi Province. This poem in which heaven and earth seem to merge into one reads as if it were written by an immortal or an angel fallen from on high. The first line describes the peak which looks like a censer in which incense is burned to gods or immortals, but the incense turns into wreaths of cloud in sunlight as if the mountain began to blend with Heaven. The verb to "exhale" is used to personify the peak so that the mountain may seem to evaporate into the sky. In line 2, the word "upend" is employed to show that the poet believed there was a Creator in the universe, for who could upend a stream but gods and immortals? In line 3, the verb to "dash" shows the power of the waterfall and the grandeur of the Creator. In line 4 "the Silver River" is coined to give a new image to the Milky Way. Here we see on the one hand the mountain peak going up to blend with the sky and on the other the Milky Way coming down to mingle with the earth.

As for the other characteristic of Li's poetry, we may read *A Dialogue in the Mountain* which is full of flowing grace:

> *I dwell among green hills and someone asks me why,*
> *My mind carefree, I smile and give him no reply.*
> *Peach blossoms fallen on running water pass by,*
> *This is an earthly paradise beneath the sky.*

This quatrain reads as smooth as the running water with peach blossoms fallen on it. It is a dialogue without an answer. The first line is a question; the second shows the poet's love of freedom, the third his love of nature, and the last his love of beauty and his image of paradise. This verse is full of natural grace.

Li Bai's imagery may either be sublime or graceful. One of his favorite images is the fabulous roc:

> *If once together with the wind the roc could rise,*
> *He would fly ninety thousand miles up to the skies.*
> *E'en if he must descend when the wind has abated,*
> *Still billows will be raised and the sea agitated.*

Here we may say the roc is as vigorous in body as the poet is in mind, and the giant bird symbolizes the poet's love of freedom.

Another favorite image of his is the moon, for instance, in his well-known quatrain *Thoughts on a Silent Night*:

> *Before my bed a pool of light —*
> *Is it hoarfrost upon the ground?*
> *Eyes raised, I see the moon so bright;*
> *Head bent, in homesickness I'm drowned.*

In the last line, the verb to "drown" is used to compare both moonlight and homesickness to water so as to find a link of connection between them. This quatrain is as popular in China as the song *Home Sweet Home* is in the West. The words are simple, but they could arouse the feeling deep in the heart and common to the millions.

In describing natural scenery, Li's verse is characterized by a swift and fierce imaginative sweep. For instance, he writes in *Mount Skyland Ascended in a Dream*:

> *Oh! Lightning flashes*
> *And thunder rumbles*
> *With stunning crashes*
> *Peak on peak crumbles.*

Even in describing human feelings, Li Bai always compares them to natural phenomena. For instance,

> 1. *Oh! Ask the river flowing to the east, I pray,*
>   *If he is happier to go than I to stay!*
>   (*Parting at a Tavern in Jinling*)

> 2. *Like floating cloud you'll float away;*
>   *With parting day I'll part from you.*
>   (*Farewell to a Friend*)

> 3. *The Lake of Peach Blossom is a thousand fathoms deep,*
>   *But not so deep as the friendship Wang Lun and I keep.*
>   (*To Wang Lun Who Comes to Bid Me Farewell*)

In these three couplets, his friendship with common people is revealed and his parting sorrow compared to the parting day, its length to a river and its depth to a lake.

Li Bai is well-known for his friendship with Meng Haoran, for whom he has written the following quatrain *Seeing Meng Haoran Off at Yellow Crane Tower*:

> *My friend has left the west where towers Yellow Crane*
> *For River Town when willow-down and flowers reign.*
> *His lessening sail is lost in boundless azure sky,*
> *Where I see but the endless River rolling by.*

This quatrain was probably written in 728 when the twenty-eight-year-old Li Bai parted with the forty-year-old poet Meng, of whose "high value all the world is proud" and who, "white-haired, lies beneath the pine and cloud." The place where they bade farewell was Yellow Crane Tower, from where, according to the legend, an immortal flew to heaven on the back of a yellow crane. Hence, seeing an old friend off at the Tower might be associated with the immortal ascending to heaven and the white sail with the white cloud and the yellow crane. In the very beginning of this quatrain heaven and earth are joined together by the crane and a blissful atmosphere is thus created. Then the place where Meng was going was really a heaven on earth, for Yangzhou was the most prosperous city in the world during the eighth century, and the time they parted was the best season of the year. So the blissful atmosphere continued to pervade all along the river.

Then Li Bai watched his friend's ship sail farther and farther away until it vanished from view and merged into the sky. Here we seem to feel the poet's heart dilate and become boundless as the heaven. In the end, what was left before the poet was only the rolling river, and we seem to see his longing for his friend become endless as the river which also merged into the sky. The first couplet of this quatrain is a beautiful narration and the last a description of the beautiful scenery. There is not a single word about the poet's feelings, yet we can feel his heart beat with the rolling waves. Perhaps that is the reason why this quatrain is considered one of the best farewell poems in China.

In describing love between man and woman, unlike English romantic poets who are subjective, direct, profound, and elaborate, Li is objective, suggestive, subtle, and simple. We may read for instance *A Faithful Wife Longing for Her Husband in Spring*:

> *Your Northern grass must be like green silk thread;*
> *Our Western mulberries have bent their head.*
> *When your thoughts begin to turn homeward way,*
> *My heart has long been breaking night and day.*
> *To the intruding vernal wind I say:*
> *"How dare you part the curtain of my bed!"*

In this poem, Li Bai describes the tender love of a wife for her husband. The first couplet does not tell us directly that the husband has been far, far away for a long, long time, but hints at the fact that he is in the north where grass has turned green, and that his wife is left in the west where mulberry leaves have just grown thick. The second couplet is a simple contrast between their heart and thought. The third couplet is very subtle to insinuate how much the wife loves her lord and how faithful she is to him. She would not allow the wind to part her bed-curtain and intrude into her bed, let alone any human intruder. This instance shows how the Chinese poet would suggest more than express.

Even in describing sorrow, Li Bai has given little to expressions of despair or bitterness. His poetry, on the whole, is calm, at times sunny in outlook. It appears to grow out of certain convictions that he held regarding life and art out of a tireless search for spiritual freedom and communion with nature. For instance, he writes in *Hard Is the Way of the World (I)*:

A time will come to ride the wind and cleave the waves,
I'll set my cloud-white sail and cross the sea which raves.

When he felt sad, he would find consolation in drinking as he said in *Invitation to Wine*:

My fur coat worth a thousand coins of gold
And my flower-dappled horse may be sold
To buy good wine that we may drown the woe age-old.

We can see that his woe was not short-lived personal sorrow

but age-old common woe. His communion with nature may be seen in *Sitting Alone in Face of Peak Jingting*:

> *All birds have flown away, so high;*
> *A lonely cloud drifts on, so free.*
> *We are not tired, the Peak and I,*
> *Nor I of him, nor he of me.*

The words "lonely" and "free" of the second line apply not only to the cloud but also to the human spectator and to the mood of the entire poem. So we can see the communion between the poet and nature. For another example, we may read his *Leaving the White Emperor Town for Jiangling*:

> *Leaving at dawn the White Emperor crowned with cloud,*
> *I've sailed a thousand li through Canyons in a day.*
> *With monkeys' sad adieux the riverbanks are loud;*
> *My skiff has left ten thousand mountains far away.*

The White Emperor Town crowned with cloud looks like an abode for immortals. In the second line, there is a marked contrast between the long distance and the short time. To go a thousand *li* in one day's space would seem impossible in ancient China for human beings but possible only for gods and goddesses. Here we see the poet more likened to an immortal than to a man. In the third line, we hear the sad adieux of monkeys who were considered as companions of Taoist immortals. In the last line, we see the fleeting movement of a skiff which looked like a leaf used by gods or goddesses to float on water. Thus a celestial atmosphere is created in this terrestrial quatrain. That is one of the reasons why Li Bai was called a poet immortal.

Li Bai's poetry frequently contains a strong element of fantasy and the supernatural. It is known for its innovative lyrical imagery and great beauty of language. His love of nature is revealed in many poems; his love of solitude in *Sitting Alone in Face of Peak Jingting*; his love of friends in his poems for Meng Haoran, Wang Changling, Du Fu, Wang Lun, and his Elegies on Master Brewer Ji, and on his Japanese friend Abe Nakamaro; his love of children in his poem *Written for My Two Children in East Lu*; his love of drink in *Drinking Alone under the Moon*. As for his love of beauty, we may read the following verse in his *Songs of the Southern Lass*:

> *The rippling dress vies with the rippling stream,*
> *We know not which by which is beautified.*

Some of his poems deal with the love of beauty in appearance, but with political aspiration in reality, for instance, *Lovesickness*. His sympathy for the oppressed people and lonely women is shown in the *Song of the Tow-men* and *The North Wind*. On the other hand, his antipathy against the oppressing rulers is revealed in his Satire on the King of Wu and on Emperor of Qin who sought elixir of the immortality in vain. The latter ends by the following:

> *(We but see) Buried in underworld, the ashes cold*

Of Emperor of Qin in coffin made of gold!

(III)

Li Bai is the best known Chinese poet in the world. The first English version of his poetry is *The Works of Li Po* translated by Shigeyoshi Obata and published in 1922 by Dutton in New York, on which Professor Wen Yiduo wrote a critical essay in 1926. The second version is included in Arthur Waley's *The Poetry and Career of Li Po* published in 1950 by Allen & Unwin in London. The third is *Li Po and Tu Fu* translated by Arthur Cooper and published in 1973 by Penguin Books. Since 1980, many editions of Li Bai's poetry have been published in China. It is said that Li Bai has exercised influence on English romantic poets, of which I am not sure, but I think we may make a comparison between them. English poets may be symbolized by the birds they sing of, Wordsworth by the cuckoo, Coleridge by the albatross, Byron by the eagle, Shelley by the skylark, and Keats by the nightingale. Then Li Bai can be symbolized by the fabulous roc by whom "*E'en if he must descend when the wind has abated, / Still billows will be raised and the sea agitated.*" American imagists Ezra Pound and Amy Lowell were also translators of Li Bai's poetry. May I not say that they are two billows raised by the roc? Sorry to say, their translations of Li Bai failed to "build up the blue dome of air" (Shelley: *The Cloud*) where the roc has to fly, so "I arise and rebuild it again", and build a dome over the agitated sea.

许渊冲译李白诗选

访戴天山[1]道士不遇

[1] 戴天山：位于今四川省江油市西北，青年李白曾在该山中的大明寺读书。

犬吠[2]水声中，
桃花带露浓[3]。
树深时[4]见鹿，
溪午不闻钟。
野竹分青霭[5]，
飞泉挂碧峰。
无人知所去，
愁倚[6]两三松。

[2] 吠：狗叫。

[3] 带露浓：挂满了露珠。

[4] 时：有时、偶尔。

[5] 青霭：紫色的云气。

[6] 倚：靠着。

戴天山位于今四川省江油市西北，是李白青少年时期生活的地方，李白作此诗时大概还不满20岁。本诗题目虽为访人不遇，然前三联均写途中所见自然景色，最后一联才点明主旨，但细细品来，前面却又埋有"不遇"的伏笔，如"时见鹿"反衬不见人，"不闻钟"暗示道观无人。王夫之评此诗说："全不添入情事，只拈死'不遇'二字作，愈死愈活。"（《唐诗评选》）而清代吴大受则说："无一字说道士，无一字说不遇，却句句是不遇，句句是访道士不遇。"（《诗筏》）

（许渊冲译李白诗选）

Calling on a Taoist Recluse in Daitian Mountain* without Meeting Him

Dogs' barks are muffled by the rippling brook,
Peach blossoms tinged by dew much redder look.
In the thick woods a deer is seen at times;
Along the stream I hear no noonday chimes.
In the blue haze which wild bamboos divide,
Tumbling cascades hang on green mountainside.
Where has the Taoist gone? No one can tell me.
Saddened, I lean on this or that pine tree.

---

* In present-day Sichuan Province.

登锦城散花楼

日照锦城①头,
朝光散花楼。
金窗②夹绣户③,
珠箔④悬银钩。
飞梯⑤绿云中,
极目⑥散我忧。
暮雨向三峡⑦,
春江绕双流⑧。
今来一登望,
如上九天游。

① 锦城:一般指今四川省成都市。此处驻扎三国蜀汉时管理织锦之官,因此得名。后人也别称成都"锦城",又称锦里。
② 金窗:华美的窗。
③ 绣户:雕饰华美的门户。
④ 珠箔(bó):即珠帘。由珍珠串成或以珍珠作装饰的帘子。
⑤ 飞梯:指往高处攀登的一步步台阶。
⑥ 极目:尽力往目之所及之处远远眺望。
⑦ 三峡:指长江三峡。说法众多,今以瞿塘峡、巫峡、西陵峡为三峡。
⑧ 双流:县名,隶属成都府。其位置位于县在二江(郫江、流江)之间,因而名为双流,即今四川省成都市双流区。

这首诗是李白早年初游成都时所作。锦城为成都别称,散花楼为隋末蜀王杨秀所建。作者没有着重于客观事物的描写,而是通过感官的主观感受,显现出散花楼的高雅别致,宏伟壮观。"飞梯绿云中,极目散我忧",这两句看似不合格律,如果去掉这两句,此诗就相当于一首五言律诗了。然而这两句在诗中却起到了很微妙的作用,可以说是"诗眼"。以此为承接点,前半部的意象构成一幅十分鲜明的画面,后半部写出了

On the Flowery Tower in the Town of Silk*

The sun shines on the Town of Silk, the Tower
Is steeped in morning glow as strewn with flowers.
By golden windows and embroidered doors,
The pearly curtains hang on silver hooks.
Into green clouds a flight of stairways soars;
The gloom's dispelled at such sunny outlooks.
The evening rain towards Three Canyons flies;
Around the town wind rivers crystal-clear.
Today I come to feast on this my eyes
As if I visited Celestial Sphere.

诗人的快意之感,这两句显示了作者极端夸张笔法的感染力。末句"如上九天游"则是抒发登楼的愉悦之情。全诗以时间为主轴展开描述,从朝光到暮雨,并且向四周扩散,南到双流城,东至三峡,形象鲜明,意境飘逸,情景真切,开合自然。

* Present-day Chengdu, capital of Sichuan Province.

峨眉山月歌

峨眉山①月半轮秋②,
影③入平羌④江水流。
夜发⑤清溪⑥向三峡,
思君不见下⑦渝州⑧。

① 峨眉山:位于今四川省乐山市。
② 半轮秋:半圆的秋月,即上弦月或下弦月。
③ 影:月光的影子。
④ 平羌:一指青衣江,处于峨眉山东北。其源头出于四川芦山,流经乐山,汇入岷江。
⑤ 发:出发。
⑥ 清溪:指清溪驿,在峨眉山附近。
⑦ 下:顺流而下。
⑧ 渝州:治所在巴县,今重庆一带。

这首诗是公元724年李白第一次离开故乡时写的七言绝句。第一句中峨眉山月象征金黄的秋天,一弯新月有如金秋的眉毛。第二句写月影随江水东流,是顺流而下才看得到的景色。第三句写人写地,用地名来叙事。第四句抒情,句中的"君"指山月,因为山高蔽月,所以就见山不见月了。诗中把月拟人化,形象很美;离情不断如水,意境深远。这首诗的特点是用了五个地名:峨眉、平羌、清溪、三峡、渝州,"四句入地名者五,古今目为绝唱,殊不厌重"(王麟洲语)。如果把前两句的地名删掉,改成"山月半轮秋,影入江水流",没有地方色彩,不能融景入情,反而会显得一般化。而李白的长处正是把地名化在叙事、写景、抒情之中,化腐朽为神奇。

The Moon over the Eyebrow Mountains[*]

The crescent moon looks like old Autumn's golden brow,
Its deep reflection flows with limpid water blue.
I'll leave the town on Clear Stream for Three Canyons now.
O Moon, how I miss you when you are out of view![†]

---

[*] In present-day Sichuan Province.
[†] The moon was screened from view by the riverside cliffs.

巴①女词

①巴：今四川巴江一带，旧时为巴国。巴女，巴地的女子。

巴水②急如箭，
巴船去若飞。
十月三千里，
郎行几岁归？

②巴水：水名，在湖北省境内。巴水：指三峡中的长江水，因处在三巴之地，因而得名。王琦注："唐之渝州、涪州、忠州、万州等处，皆古时巴郡。其水流经三峡下至夷陵。当盛涨时，箭飞之速，不足过矣。"

此诗是李白第一次出川在嘉陵江流域游历时模仿当地民歌所作，故颇有民谣风格。诗从巴水写起，转而抒发思念之苦，眼见巴水急如箭，眼见巴船去如飞，而所念之人仍在天涯。出行已是过了十月，叹逝者如斯之快；行程则三千里了，叹沧海碣石之远。一快一远，无解的一问，留给读者的是无尽的思念和遐想。

Song of a Woman of Ba*

The River fast like arrow flows;
Your boat as if on wings swift goes.
Ten months, a thousand miles away.
When will you come back? On what day?

---

* Present-day Sichuan Province.

荆 州 歌[1]

白帝城边足[2]风波,
瞿塘[3]五月谁敢过?
荆州麦熟茧[4]成蛾,
缲丝[5]忆君头绪[6]多。
拨谷飞鸣奈妾何[7]?

[1] 荆州歌:古题乐府杂曲歌辞。《乐府诗集》卷七十二列于《杂曲歌辞》,又名"荆州乐""江陵乐"。《乐府诗集·杂曲歌辞十二·荆州乐》郭茂倩题解:《荆州乐》盖出于《清商曲·江陵乐》,荆州即江陵也。有纪南城,在江陵县东。梁建文帝《荆州歌》云"纪城南里望朝云,雉飞麦熟妾思君"是也。

[2] 足:充足,诗中理解为满是,都是。

[3] 瞿(qú)塘:即瞿塘峡,与巫峡、西陵峡共称长江三峡。

[4] 茧(jiǎn):指蚕茧。

[5] 缲(sāo)丝:即缫丝,将蚕茧抽出蚕丝的工艺。在南朝乐府中"丝""思"为双关语。

[6] 头绪:也说思绪。

[7] 拨谷飞鸣奈妾何:写思妇默念:拨谷鸟已鸣,春天将尽,不见夫回,使人无可奈何。拨谷:即布谷鸟。布谷叫,也表明农忙季节已到。

此作中民间生活气息很浓,"足风波""谁敢过""头绪多""奈妾何",就是民间口语的直接化用。全诗写的是一位农村妇女辛勤劳作之时思念远方丈夫的愁苦情景。白帝城边的江面上满是狂风掀起的惊涛骇浪,五月的瞿塘峡,江流湍急,暗礁丛生,归路受阻。思妇在家,眼看麦已成熟,春蚕也已经破茧成蛾,忙碌地缲着丝,触景生情涌起心中的"思",叫人千头万绪。布谷鸟飞来飞去,在头上叫个不停。诗人以敏锐的笔触,生动形象地刻画了这丰富、复杂、微妙的情感,恰到好处地勾画出了女主人公复杂而又强烈的思念之情。

The Silk Spinner

The White King* Town's seen many shipwrecks on the sands.

Who dare to sail through Three Canyons in the fifth moon?

The wheat is ripe; the silkworm has made its cocoon.

My thoughts of you are endless as the silken strands.

The cuckoos sing: "Go Home!"

When will you come to homeland?

---

* Or the White Emperor Town in present-day Sichuan Province, situated on the northern shore of the Changjiang (Yangtze) River.

渡荆门[1]送别

[1] 荆门：山名，现今湖北省宜昌市宜都市西北长江南岸，与北岸虎牙山对峙，地势险要，自古以来被称为楚蜀咽喉。

渡远[2]荆门外，
来从楚国[3]游。
山随平野[4]尽，
江[5]入大荒[6]流。
月下飞天镜[7]，
云生结海楼[8]。
仍怜故乡水，
万里送行舟。

[2] 远：远自。
[3] 楚国：楚地，指湖北一带，春秋时期属楚国。
[4] 平野：平坦开阔的原野。
[5] 江：长江。
[6] 大荒：广阔无垠的田野。
[7] 月下飞天镜：月光洒在江水上，如同飞下的天镜。
[8] 海楼：海市蜃楼，这里形容江上的云霞异常美丽。

《渡荆门送别》是公元725年李白乘船出三峡时写的五言律诗。诗人离开了荆门山，看见三峡的高山峻岭换成了广阔的平原，滚滚的江水流向茫茫的远方。到了夜间，一轮明月飞下天空，犹如明镜，片片白云升起，仿佛海市蜃楼，这和故乡的峨眉山月大异其趣。但是长江之波还是故乡流来的水，水波依依不舍地追随着诗人远行万里。这样，年轻的诗人就使无情的山水也富有诗情画意。李白诗的特点正是借景写情，使景语都变成情语了。

Farewell Beyond the Thorn-Gate Gorge*

Leaving Mount Thorn-Gate far away,
My boat pursues its eastward way.
Where mountains end begins the plain;
The river rolls to boundless main.
The moon, celestial mirror, flies;
The clouds like miraged towers rise.
The water that from homeland flows
Will follow me where my boat goes.

---

* In present-day Hubei Province.

望庐山瀑布水

（二首其二）

日照香炉①生紫烟，
遥看②瀑布挂③前川④。
飞流直⑤下三千尺⑥，
疑⑦是银河落九天⑧。

① 香炉，指香炉峰，庐山北部名峰。紫烟，指日光穿过云雾，远远望去像紫色的烟云。

② 遥看：远看。

③ 挂：悬挂。

④ 川：河流，这里指瀑布。

⑤ 直：笔直。

⑥ 三千尺：形容山高。这里使用了夸张的手法。

⑦ 疑：怀疑。

⑧ 九天：形容天高。古人认为天有九重，九天是天的最高层，九重天，即天空最高处。

　　这是公元726年李白游庐山时的作品。巍巍的香炉峰上白云缭绕，在红日照耀下形成一片紫霞，仿佛冉冉上升的烟雾。远远看去，瀑布像一匹巨大的白练高挂在山川之间。在青山的衬托之下，云烟似乎也成了四溅的水珠，瀑布显得更高更陡，喷涌而出，飞奔而下，简直就像银河从天而降。这种浪漫主义的想象使这首小诗令人神往。宋人魏庆之说："七言诗第五字要响。"这首诗第一句的"生"、第二句的"挂"、第四句的"落"都是动词，非常响亮，如果换掉这三个字，气势就没有这样磅礴了。

The Waterfall in Mount Lu* Viewed from Afar
(II)

The sunlit Censer Peak exhales incense-like cloud,
The cataract hangs like upended stream sounding loud.
Its torrent dashes down three thousand feet from high
As if the Silver River† fell from azure sky.

---

* Or the Lu Mountains in present-day Jiangxi Province.
† The Chinese name for the Milky Way.

望庐山五老峰[①]

[①] 五老峰：庐山东南部由五座形似老人的雄奇峰岭连结而成的山峰，山势险峻，是庐山胜景之一。李白曾在此地筑舍读书。

庐山东南五老峰，
青天削出金芙蓉[②]。
九江秀色[③]可揽结[④]，
吾将此地巢云松[⑤]。

[②] 金芙蓉：莲花的美称。
[③] 秀色：秀丽的风景。
[④] 揽结：收集，拮取。
[⑤] 巢云松：隐居此处。

此作体现了诗人一贯的浪漫主义情怀。这首诗是一首吟咏美景的佳作，五老峰坐落在庐山的东南面，因山势险峻，五峰相连，形似五位老人，因而得名。起句"庐山东南五老峰"，一下笔就触及题旨，第二句的"削"字极妙，极言山峰的耸立险峻之状。登山俯瞰山下九江秀丽景色，似乎可以随手采到一样，难怪诗人触动情肠不忍离去，有了避世隐居的想法。纵览全诗，浪漫色彩的想象、趣味的夸张，使一幅美景跃然纸上，所以说这不仅是一首写景诗，更是作者对自然的热爱之情的流露。

The Five Greybeard-like Peaks of Mount Lu Viewed from Afar

Southeast of Mountain Lu, Five Peaks of Greybeard stand
As golden lotus carved by Heaven's azure hand.
If I could drink in beauty of the Rivers Nine*,
Here I would build my nest amid the cloud and pine.

---

* Jiujiang means nine rivers in present-day Jiangxi Province.

望天门山①

① 天门山：在今安徽省马鞍山市当涂县西南长江两岸，东为东梁山（也称博望山），西为西梁山（又也称梁山）。两山隔江对立，仿佛天设的门户一般，故名。

天门中断②楚江③开④，
碧水东流至此⑤回⑥。
两岸青山⑦相对出，
孤帆一片日边来⑧。

② 中断：江水从中间隔断两山。
③ 楚江：长江流经旧楚地故称楚江。
④ 开：横断开来。
⑤ 至此：意为东流的江水流至此处转向北流。
⑥ 回：回漩，回转。指水流由于流向突变湍急起来。
⑦ 两岸青山：分别指东梁山和西梁山。
⑧ 日边来：指孤舟从天水相接处的远方驶来，远远望去，仿佛来自日边。

　　天门山是安徽东西梁山的合称，两山隔江对峙，好像天开的门户，所以叫天门山。山居然给长江冲断了，可见水势汹涌；水势虽猛，到此还是不得不改变流向，可见山势险峻。诗人乘船顺流而下，峰回路转，仿佛两岸青山争相迎接。一个"出"字，把山都写活了。"孤帆一片"，究竟是望中的孤舟，还是诗人坐的船呢？如是望中的孤舟，那么，"日"应该是朝阳；如指诗人的船，则是夕阳。从全诗来看，还是青山迎接诗人更好。如果诗中无人，这首诗就纯粹是写景；如果有人，那才更能融景入情。

Mount Heaven's Gate* Viewed from Afar

Breaking Mount Heaven's Gate, the great River rolls through,
Its east-flowing green billows, hurled back here, turn north.
From the two river banks thrust out the mountains blue,
Leaving the sun behind, a lonely sail comes forth.

* In present-day Anhui Province.

杨叛儿①

① 杨叛儿：一作"阳叛儿"，原为南北朝时的童谣，后来成为乐府诗题。《乐府诗集》卷四十九列为《清商曲辞》。

君歌②杨叛儿，
妾劝新丰酒③。
何许④最关人⑤？
乌啼白门⑥柳。
乌啼隐⑦杨花，
君醉留妾家。
博山炉⑧中沉香⑨火，
双烟一气⑩凌紫霞⑪。

② 君歌：即"君家"。
③ 新丰酒：原指在长安新丰镇生产的酒。此指江南之新丰酒。
④ 何许：何处，哪里。
⑤ 关人：牵动人的情思。
⑥ 白门：刘宋都城建康（今南京）城门。
⑦ 隐：隐没，这里指乌鸦栖息在杨花丛中。
⑧ 博山炉：古香炉名。
⑨ 沉香：又名沉水香，一种可燃的名贵香料。
⑩ 双烟一气：两股烟缭绕在一起，用以形容男女两情之合好如一。
⑪ 紫霞：指天空云霞。

　　这首诗取材于乐府《杨叛儿》。一对青年男女，君唱歌，妾劝酒，一开头就呈现出一对恋人互相爱慕的美好画面，愉悦的气氛贯穿全诗。白门即刘宋都城建康（今南京）城门。南朝民间情歌常常提到白门，后代指男女欢会之地。对热恋之中的人来说，最牵动人心的自然是约会的时间和地点，"乌啼"即指日暮，对"何许最关人"这一设问，无疑"乌啼白门柳"道出了所有恋人的心声。乌啼是薄暮，乌隐是迟暮，恋人陶醉在甜情蜜意中，一醉一留间，将爱情表现得尤为炽烈。此句意境动人，与"月上柳梢头，人约黄昏后"有异曲同工之妙。最后两句蕴含道教哲学的绝妙比喻，使全诗得到升华，这是一首唯美的爱情之诗。

A Love Song

You sing a lover's lore;
I urge you to drink more.
What touches you and me?
Crow's nest in willow tree.
Crows hide mid poplar flowers;
Drunk, you stay in my bowers.
Behold the censer and the sandalwood in fire!
Two wreaths of smoke combine and rise higher and higher.

长 干 行[①]

（二首其一）

①长干行：属乐府《杂曲歌辞》调名。

妾发初覆额，

折花门前剧。

郎骑竹马来，

绕床[②]弄青梅。

同居长干里[③]，

两小无嫌猜。

十四为君妇，

羞颜未尝开。

低头向暗壁，

千唤不一回。

十五始展眉，

愿同尘与灰。

②床：井栏，即后院围住水井的栅栏。

③长干里：位于今南京市，旧时船民多聚居于此，因而《长干曲》多抒发船家女子的感情。

《长干行》是李白爱情诗的代表作，写长干里的少年儿女青梅竹马，后来结为夫妇，但愿共甘苦同生死。丈夫愿学在桥下约会的情人，等到水涨女方还没来时，宁愿抱着桥柱淹死也不离开。现在丈夫出外经商，三峡水急滩险，经常船沉人亡，连猿猴都悲啼哀鸣了。妻子在门前等候，像

Ballads of a Merchant's Wife

(I)

My forehead covered by my hair cut straight,

I played with flowers plucked before the gate.

On a hobbyhorse you came upon the scene,

Around the well we played with mumes still green.

We lived close neighbors on riverside lane.

Carefree and innocent, we children twain.

I was fourteen when I became your bride;

I'd often turn my bashful face aside.

Hanging my head, I'd look towards the wall;

A thousand times I'd not answer your call.

I was fifteen when I composed my brows;

To mix my dust with yours were my dear vows.

在望夫台上,一直等到台阶上长满了绿苔,蝴蝶也变老了,丈夫还没回家。她不免感到悲哀,希望他能早从三峡归来,先寄一封家信,她会不怕路远,到几百里外的长风沙去接他。这是古代借相思写爱情的代表作。

常存抱柱信①,
岂上望夫台!
十六君远行,
瞿塘滟滪堆②。
五月不可触,
猿声天上哀。
门前迟行迹,
一一生绿苔。
苔深不能扫,
落叶秋风早。
八月蝴蝶黄,
双飞西园草。
感此伤妾心,
坐愁红颜老。
早晚③下三巴④,
预将书报家。
相迎不道远,
直至长风沙⑤。

① 抱柱信:典出《庄子·盗跖篇》,写尾生与一女子相约于桥下见面,女子未到却突然涨水,尾生因守信不愿离去,抱着柱子被水淹死。

② 滟(yàn)滪(yù)堆:三峡之一瞿塘峡峡口的一块大礁石,农历五月涨水没礁,过往船只极易触礁沉没。

③ 早晚:什么时候。

④ 三巴:地名。即巴郡、巴东、巴西。在今四川东部地区。

⑤ 长风沙:地名,在今安徽省安庆市的长江沿岸,距南京约700里。

Rather than break faith, you declared you'd die.
Who knew I'd live alone in a tower high?
I was sixteen when you went far away,
Passing Three Canyons studded with rocks grey,
Where ships were wrecked when spring flood ran high,
Where gibbons' wails seemed coming from the sky.
Green moss now overgrows before our door;
Your footprints, hidden, can be seen no more.
Moss can't be swept away: so thick it grows,
And leaves fall early when the west wind blows.
The yellow butterflies in autumn pass
Two by two o'er our western garden grass.
This sight would break my heart, and I'm afraid,
Sitting alone, my rosy cheeks would fade.
Sooner or later, you'll leave the western land.
Do not forget to let me know beforehand.
I'll walk to meet you and not call it far
To go to Long Wind Sands or where you are.

长干行

（二首其二）

忆妾①深闺里，
烟尘不曾识。
嫁与长干人，
沙头②候风色。
五月南风兴，
思君下③巴陵。
八月西风起，
想君发④扬子。
去来悲如何，
见少离别多。

① 妾：作"昔"。

② 沙头：沙岸。

③ 下：作"在"。

④ 发：出发。

如果说第一首诗从各个生活阶段的各个生活侧面着手，塑造出一个对理想生活执着追求和热切向往的商贾思妇的艺术形象，那么第二首则从商妇望夫说起，感情层层深入，直至自怜自恨而止，抒写妻子对外出远商的丈夫的挚爱和思念，凄切幽怨，缠绵感人。评论界普遍认为，第二首比第一首稍逊一筹，第二首与其他闺怨诗一样直接从幽怨的少妇下

Ballads of a Merchant's Wife

(II)

Brought up while young in inner room,

I knew nor wind nor dust that rose.

Since you became my dear bridegroom,

I've learned on Sands from where wind blows.

In the fifth moon south wind is high,

I know you're sailing the river down;

In the eighth moon west wind comes nigh,

I think you'll leave the river town.

I'm grieved to see you come and go:

We sever longer than we meet.

笔,第一首自出机杼从童年时两小无猜写起。其实,第一首呈现的是一幅幅生活场景,着重刻画人物性格,满腹相思还未倾诉,这就引出了第二首。如果说第一首是清水出芙蓉的水墨画,那么第二首就是色彩浓得化不开的油画,满纸都是浓浓的相思。

湘潭^①几日到?
妾梦越风波!
昨夜狂风度,
吹折江头树。
淼淼^②暗无边,
行人在何处?
好乘浮云骢^③,
佳期兰渚^④东。
鸳鸯绿蒲上,
翡翠^⑤锦屏中。
自怜十五余,
颜色桃花红。
那作商人妇,
愁水复愁风!

① 湘潭:泛指湖南一带。

② 淼淼:形容水势浩大。

③ 浮云骢(cōng):骏马。西汉文帝有骏马名浮云。

④ 兰渚:长有兰草的小洲。

⑤ 翡翠:水鸟名。

When will you come home? Let me know!

To cross the waves my dream is fleet.

Last night a violent wind blew,

Breaking the trees by riverside.

So dark the boundless waters grew!

Where could your roving ship abide?

I'd ride upon a cloud-like steed

To meet you east of River Green

Like two love birds amid the reed

Or kingfishers on silken screen.

I pity my fifteen odd years,

Like blooming peach my face is warm.

But I'm a merchant's wife in tears,

Who worries over wind and storm.

金陵酒肆[①]留别

[①] 酒肆：酒店。

风吹柳花满店香，
吴姬压酒劝客尝。
金陵子弟[②]来相送，
欲行[③]不行[④]各尽觞[⑤]。
请君试问东流水，
别意与之谁短长？

[②] 子弟：指李白的朋友。

[③] 欲行：即将离开的人，指诗人自己。

[④] 不行：不走的人，指送别的人。

[⑤] 尽觞（shāng）：一口喝完杯中的酒。觞，酒杯。

公元726年暮春时节，柳絮飘飞，李白离开金陵到扬州去。青年朋友到酒店来送行，店中女郎从酒糟中压出酒来，劝客人多喝几杯。将行的人和送行的人都开怀畅饮，于是李白就写下了这首小诗。他要问问长江的流水，到底是江水更高兴流走，还是他更高兴留下呢？全诗没有一个"愁"字，因为生活中没有愁，所以诗中就只有别情，无怪乎沈德潜说"语不必深，写情已足"。

Parting at a Tavern in Jinling*

The tavern's sweetened when wind blows in willow-down;
A Southern maiden bids the guests to taste the wine.
My dear young friends have come to see me leave the town;
They drink their cups and I, still tarrying, drink mine.
Oh! Ask the river flowing to the east, I pray,
If he is happier to go than I to stay!

* Present-day Nanjing, capital of Jiangsu Province.

夜下征虏亭[1]

[1] 征虏亭：东晋时征虏将军谢石所建，故址在今江苏省南京市南郊。此诗题下原注："《丹阳记》：亭是太安中征虏将军谢安所立，因以为名。"据《晋书·谢安传》等史料，谢安从未有过征虏将军的封号，这里"谢安"应是"谢石"之误。

船下广陵去，
月明征虏亭。
山花如绣颊[2]，
江火[3]似流萤[4]。

[2] 绣颊(jiá)：女子脸颊涂上胭脂后，色如锦绣，因称绣颊。此处借喻岸上山花的娇艳。
[3] 江火：江上的渔火。
[4] 流萤：飞舞的萤火虫。

这首诗应该是李白写了《金陵酒肆留别》之后，上船到扬州去，在月下经过征虏亭时写的。诗人把烂漫的山花比作天真烂漫、巧妆打扮的妙龄少女的脸颊，把长江两岸星星点点的万家灯火比作闪闪烁烁的万点萤光，画出了一幅令人心醉神迷的春江花月图。英译文把每句诗的五个字译成八个音节（四个抑扬格的音步），来传达这首小诗的意美、音美和形美。

Passing by the Triumphal Tower at Night

My boat sails down to River Town*,
The Tower's bright in the moonlight.
The flowers blow like cheeks that glow,
And lanterns beam as fireflies gleam.

---

* Yangzhou in Jiangsu Province.

上①李邕

① 上：呈上。

大鹏一日同风起，
扶摇②直上九万里。
假令③风歇时下来，
犹能簸却④沧溟水。
世人见我恒⑤殊调⑥，
闻⑦余大言皆冷笑。
宣父⑧犹能畏后生，
丈夫⑨未可轻年少。

② 扶摇：乘风。摇，由下而上的大风。
③ 假令：假使，即使。
④ 簸却：激起。
⑤ 恒：总，经常。
⑥ 殊调：不寻常的论调，不同世俗的言行。
⑦ 闻：作"见"。
⑧ 宣父：孔子，唐太宗贞观十一年（637年）诏尊孔子为宣父。
⑨ 丈夫：古代男子的通称，这里指李邕。

这首诗是李白青年时期的作品。李邕于开元七至九年（719—721）前后任渝州（今重庆）刺史，李白游渝州拜见李邕，希望通过李邕引荐找到政治出路，却因不拘俗礼，且谈论间放言高论，纵谈王霸，使李邕不悦，受到冷遇，愤激之余写下此诗，以示回敬。但由于李邕年辈长于李白，故诗题云"上"。前四句中李白以大鹏自比，大鹏鸟是庄子哲学中自由的象征、理想的图腾。观李白诗作，不难发现其受道家哲学影响之深，而正是由于道教哲学的影响，才造就了李白的旷达飘逸、奇思妙想。诗的前四句既勾画出了一个力簸沧海的大鹏形象，也是诗人对自己形象的描述。后四句则是对李邕的傲慢态度的直接回敬，不同凡响的言论不被凡夫俗子理解，孔子尚且说过"后生可畏"，谁又能轻视年轻人呢？这是揶揄，是讽刺，青年李白就已展示了过人的胆识。

The Roc— to Li Yong[*]

If once together with the wind the roc could rise,

He would fly ninety thousand miles up to the skies.

E'en if he must descend when the wind has abated,

Still billows will be raised and the sea agitated.

Seeing me, those in power think I'm rather queer;

Hearing me freely talk, they can't refrain from sneer.

Confucius was in dread of talents that would be;

A sage will ne'er look down upon a youth like me.

---

[*] In 726 Li Bai sought the patronage of Li Yong, an official who was more than twenty years older than him.

静 夜 思[1]

[1] 静夜思：在安静夜晚所产生的思绪。

床前明月光，
疑[2]是地上霜。
举头[3]望明月，
低头思故乡。

[2] 疑：好像。

[3] 举头：抬头。

《静夜思》是李白传诵最广的名诗。第一句"床前明月光"，有人说"床"应该是井床，"明月"应该是山月，但一般都理解为卧室的床前，英译文就从众了。因为明月是圆的，会引起中国人团圆的思想，这就是《静夜思》的主题。但西方人并没有团圆的观念，天上的圆月也不会使人想到家人的团圆。因此，译文第一行把明月光比作水，说是一池月光；第四行又说沉浸在乡愁中，再把乡愁也比作水。这样就用水，而不是用圆，把明月和乡愁联系起来了。

Thoughts on a Silent Night

Before my bed a pool of light —
Is it hoarfrost upon the ground?
Eyes raised, I see the moon so bright;
Head bent, in homesickness I'm drowned.

黄鹤楼①送孟浩然之②广陵③

① 黄鹤楼：故址在今湖北省武汉市武昌蛇山的黄鹤矶上，属于长江下游地带，传说三国时期的费祎于此登仙乘黄鹤而去，故称黄鹤楼。孟浩然：李白的朋友。

② 之：到。

③ 广陵：扬州。

故人④西辞⑤黄鹤楼，
烟花⑥三月下扬州。
孤帆远影碧空尽⑦，
唯见⑧长江天际流⑨。

④ 故人：老朋友，此处指孟浩然。其年龄比李白大，在诗坛上颇具盛名。李白对其非常钦佩，彼此感情深厚，因此称之为"故人"。

⑤ 辞：辞别。

⑥ 烟花：扬州柳絮飘荡和琼花美艳绝伦，这里指扬州绝美的春景。

⑦ 碧空尽：消失在碧蓝的天际。尽：尽头，消失了。碧空：一作"碧山"。

⑧ 唯见：只见。

⑨ 天际流：向天边流去。天际：天边，天边的尽头。

许渊冲译李白诗选

这首七绝是李白在一个繁华时代的繁华季节，送孟浩然去一个繁华地方的送别诗。诗中第一句的黄鹤楼，是传说中仙人驾鹤升天的地方，这会使人联想到孟浩然也是去人间天堂的广陵（今天的扬州），诗意就更浓了。第二句是千古丽句，写长江两岸杨柳如烟、鲜花似锦的美景，画意又增加了诗情。后两句更是融情于景。第三句表面上写的是孤帆远影，实际上说的是诗人的心已随友人远去了。第四句写的是天际江流，说的是诗人情思悠悠，无穷无尽。所以这是一首诗中有画、画中有诗的杰作。

Seeing Meng Haoran off at Yellow Crane Tower[*]

My friend has left the west where towers Yellow Crane
For River Town[†] when willow-down and flowers reign.
His lessening sail is lost in boundless azure sky,
Where I see but the endless River rolling by.

[*] In Wuhan, capital of Hubei Province.
[†] Yangzhou in Jiangsu Province.

长相思①

（二首其一）

① 长相思：属乐府《杂曲歌辞》，常以"长相思"三字开头和结尾。

长相思，
在长安。
络纬②秋啼金井阑，
微霜凄凄簟③色寒。
孤灯不明④思欲绝，
卷帷望月空长叹。
美人如花隔云端。
上有青冥⑤之高天，
下有渌⑥水之波澜。
天长地远魂飞苦，
梦魂不到关山难⑦。
长相思，
摧心肝！

② 络纬：昆虫名，又名莎鸡，俗称纺织娘。
③ 簟：可用于坐卧的竹席。
④ 不明：作"不寐"，也说"不眠"。
⑤ 青冥：青色天空。
⑥ 渌：清澈。
⑦ 关山难：关山难渡。

《长相思》共两首，都是写相思之作。这一首以秋声秋景起兴，写男子思念女子。所思美人，远在长安。天高地远，关山阻遏，梦魂难越。或以为此诗别有寄托，"美人如花隔云端"含有托兴意味，古代经常用"美人"比喻所追求之理想。而长安这个地点，当时的都城，更是赋予了此诗政治上的寓意。诗意牵涉政治虽然有些含蓄，但仍不乏诗人一贯的豪迈飘逸。

Lovesickness

(I)

I yearn for one
Who's in Chang'an*
In autumn crickets wail beside the golden rail;
The first frost, although light, invades the bed's delight.
My lonely lamp burns dull, of longing I would die;
Rolling up screens to view the moon, in vain I sigh.
My flower-like Beauty is high
Up as clouds in the sky.
Above, the boundless heaven blue is seen;
Below, the endless river rolls its billows green.
My soul can't fly o'er sky so vast nor earth so wide;
In dreams I can't go through mountain pass to her side.
We are so far apart,
The yearning breaks my heart.

---

* The Tang capital.

长 相 思

（二首其二）

日色欲尽花含烟，
月明如素①愁不眠。
赵瑟②初停凤凰柱，
蜀琴③欲奏鸳鸯弦。
此曲有意无人传，
愿随春风寄燕然④。
忆君迢迢隔青天。
昔时横波⑤目，
今作流泪泉。
不信妾肠断，
归来看取明镜前！

① 素：洁白的绢。

② 赵瑟：指弦乐器，相传古代赵国人擅长奏瑟。

③ 蜀琴：指弦乐器，古人诗中提及蜀琴俱是佳琴。

④ 燕然：山名，即杭爱山，位于今蒙古人民共和国境内。此处泛指塞北地区。

⑤ 横波：指眼睛如横波一般，非常晶莹美丽。

这一首写女子对从征戍边的丈夫的思念。作为艺术创新，诗人打破了以"长相思"一语发端的固定格式。开篇虽是春夜春景，相思之愁苦却不减反增。女主人公鼓瑟弹琴，寄思念之情于音律，然思念成空，泪如泉涌，结尾悠远绵长。

Lovesickness

(II)

Flowers exhale thin mist when daylight fades away;
The sleepless feel sad to see the moon shed silken ray.
My harp on phoenix-holder has just become mute,
I'll try to play upon lovebird strings of my lute.
My song's a message.
Who will carry it to you?
I'd ask spring wind to bear it up to the frontiers.
Between you and me there is the boundless blue sky.
Do you remember my wave-like eyes of days gone by?
Now they become a spring of tears.
If you do not believe my heart is broken, alas!
Come back and look into my bright mirror of brass!

登新平①楼

① 新平：唐朝郡名，又是县名。新平郡即邠州，治新平县。

去国②登兹楼，
怀归伤暮秋。
天长落日远，
水净寒波流。
秦云③起岭树，
胡雁④飞沙洲。
苍苍⑤几万里，
目极⑥令人愁。

② 去国：离开国都。

③ 秦云：秦地的云。新平等地先秦时属秦国。

④ 胡雁：北方的大雁。胡，古代北方少数民族的通称，这里借指北方地区。

⑤ 苍苍：一片深青色，形容旷远苍茫的样子。

⑥ 目极：指向远处眺望。

此诗作于李白第一次离开长安时。开元十八年（730），李白在长安自夏至秋，谋求仕途未成，遂于暮秋时节从长安出发踏上了西游的道路。途经邠州时，诗人登上了矗立于新平原上的城楼，四周眺望，触景生情。邠地暮秋的景象，使人百感交集。诗人通过景物渲染，抒发了寓居他乡壮志难酬的孤独凄凉之感。"苍苍几万里，目极令人愁"，诗人极目环眺，视力所及，不知安身立命何处。都城虽然并不遥远，但对于"愿做帝王辅弼"的李白来说却是遥不可及的，所有这些，千头万绪，不觉无边愁绪油然而生。

Ascending Xinping Tower[*]

Leaving the capital, I climb this tower.
Can I return home like late autumn flower?
The sky is vast, the setting sun is far;
The water clear, the waves much colder are.
Clouds rise above the western-mountain trees;
O'er river dunes fly south-going wild geese.
The boundless land outspread 'neath gloomy skies.
How gloomy I feel while I strain my eyes!

[*] In present-day Shaanxi Province.

蜀道难①

噫吁嚱②,
危乎高哉!
蜀道之难,
难于上青天!
蚕丛及鱼凫③,
开国何茫然④!
尔来⑤四万八千岁⑥,
不与秦塞⑦通人烟⑧。
西当⑨太白有鸟道⑩,
可以横绝⑪峨眉巅。

① 蜀道难:南朝乐府旧题,属《相和歌·瑟调曲》。
② 噫(yī)吁(xū)嚱(xī):惊叹声,蜀方言,表示吃惊。
③ 蚕丛、鱼凫(fú):传说是古蜀国两位国王之名,但无从取证。
④ 何茫然:何,多么。茫然,完全不知道的样子。指对传说中古代历史悠远难详,不甚了解。
⑤ 尔来:自那时以来。
⑥ 四万八千岁:表示时间漫长,此处手法夸张。
⑦ 秦塞(sài):指秦地。秦地四周山川险阻,故称"四塞之地"。
⑧ 通人烟:人员来往。
⑨ 西当:在西边的。当:在。
⑩ 鸟道:指连绵高山间的隙口,只有鸟能飞过,人迹不能至此。
⑪ 横绝:横越。

《蜀道难》是李白首屈一指的名篇,大约是公元730年他第一次到长安时写的。如果说《长相思》是借美人写慕君之情,那《蜀道难》就是借山川之景来抒写报国无门之心了。蜀道指的是上长安的青云路,所以诗一开始,诗人长吁短叹,先用神话传说写开国之难。接着写山川险峻,连黄鹤都不能飞过太白峰,暗示自己不能青云直上。又写青泥岭盘旋曲折,暗示仕途艰难,诗人只有抚胸长叹。再借"问君"引

Hard Is the Road to Shu*

Oho! Behold!

How steep!

How high!

The road to Shu is harder than to climb to the sky.

Since the two pioneers

Put the kingdom in order,

Have passed forty-eight thousand years,

And few have tried to pass its border.

There's a bird track o'er Great White Mountain to the west,

Which cuts through Mountain Eyebrows by the crest.

出旅愁:"连峰去天不盈尺",形容山峰之高;"枯松倒挂倚绝壁",衬托绝壁之险。然后由静入动,写水石激荡、山谷轰鸣。最后写到剑阁,其实是借喻朝廷要津,所守非人,必为祸害。朝避猛虎,夕避长蛇,也是借喻朝廷上下的恶势力。所以这是一首借景写情的政治抒怀诗。

* Present-day Sichuan Province.

地崩山摧壮士死①,
然后天梯②石栈③相钩连。
上有六龙回日④之高标,
下有冲波⑤逆折⑥之回川⑦。
黄鹤之飞尚不得过,
猿猱⑧欲度愁攀援。
青泥⑨何盘盘⑩,
百步九折⑪萦⑫岩峦⑬。
扪参历井⑭仰胁息⑮,
以手抚膺⑯坐⑰长叹。
问君西游何时还?
畏途⑱巉岩⑲不可攀。
但见悲鸟号古木,
雄飞雌从绕林间。
又闻子规啼夜月,
愁空山。
蜀道之难,
难于上青天,
使人听此凋朱颜。

① 地崩山摧壮士死:《华阳国志·蜀志》: 相传秦惠王想征服蜀国, 知道蜀王好色, 答应送给他五个美女。蜀王派五位壮士去接人。回到梓潼的时候, 看见一条大蛇进入穴中, 一位壮士抓住了它的尾巴, 其余四人也来相助, 用力往外拽。不多时, 山崩地裂, 壮士和美女都被压死。
② 天梯: 异常陡峭的山路。
③ 石栈(zhàn): 栈道。
④ 六龙回日:《淮南子》注云: "日乘车, 驾以六龙。羲和御之。日至此面而薄于虞渊, 羲和至此而六螭", 意思就是传说中的羲和驾驶着六龙之车(即太阳)到此处便迫近虞渊(传说中的日落处)。
⑤ 冲波: 水流冲击腾起的波浪, 这里指激流。
⑥ 逆折: 水流回旋。
⑦ 回川: 有漩涡的河流。
⑧ 猿猱(náo): 蜀山中最善攀援的猴类。
⑨ 青泥: 青泥岭, 在今甘肃徽县南, 陕西略阳县北。
⑩ 盘盘: 形容道路回旋曲折的样子。
⑪ 百步九折: 形容道路极其曲折。
⑫ 萦(yíng): 盘绕。
⑬ 岩峦: 山峰。
⑭ 扪(mén)参(shēn)历井: 参、井是二星宿名。扪, 用手摸。历, 经过。
⑮ 胁息: 屏住呼吸。
⑯ 膺(yīng): 胸。
⑰ 坐: 徒, 空。
⑱ 畏途: 可怕的路途。
⑲ 巉(chán)岩: 指山壁高耸陡峭。

The crest crumbled, five serpent-killing heroes slain,
Along the cliffs a rocky path was hacked then.
Above stand peaks too high for the sun to pass o'er;
Below the torrents run back and forth, churn and roar.
Even the Golden Crane can't fly across;
How to climb over, gibbons are at a loss.
What tortuous mountain path Green Mud Ridge faces!
Around the top we turn nine turns each hundred paces.
Looking up breathless, I can touch the stars nearby;
Beating my breast, I sink aground with long, long sigh.
When will you come back from this journey to the west?
How can you climb up dangerous path and mountain crest,
Where you can hear on ancient trees but sad birds wail
And see the female birds fly, followed by the male?
And hear home-going cuckoos weep
Beneath the moon in mountains deep?
The road to Shu is harder than to climb to the sky,
On hearing this, your cheeks would lose their rosy dye.

连峰去①天不盈尺,

枯松倒挂倚绝壁。

飞湍②瀑流争喧豗③,

砯崖④转石万壑雷。

其险也如此,

嗟尔远道之人胡为⑤乎来哉!

剑阁峥嵘而崔嵬⑥,

一夫当关,

万夫莫开。

所守或匪亲⑦,

化为狼与豺。

朝避猛虎,

夕避长蛇,

磨牙吮血,

杀人如麻。

锦城⑧虽云乐,

不如早还家。

蜀道之难,难于上青天,

侧身西望长咨嗟⑨!

① 去:距离。

② 飞湍(tuān):飞奔而下的急流

③ 喧豗(huī):喧闹声,这里指急流和瀑布撞击发出的巨大声响。

④ 砯(pīng)崖:水与石撞击的巨响。砯,急流冲击石壁发出的声响,这里用作动词,冲击。

⑤ 胡为:为什么。

⑥ 峥嵘、崔(cuī)嵬(wéi):都是形容山势雄伟高峻的样子。

⑦ 或匪(fěi)亲:假使不是值得信赖的人。匪,同"非"。

⑧ 锦城:古代成都以产棉闻名,朝廷曾经在此设官,收购棉织品,故名。

⑨ 咨(zī)嗟:叹息。

Between the sky and peaks there is not a foot's space,
And ancient pines hang, head down, from the cliff's surface,
And cataracts and torrents dash on boulders under,
Roaring like thousands of echoes of thunder.
So dangerous these places are,
Alas! Why should you come here from afar?
Rugged is the path between the cliffs so steep and high,
Guarded by one
And forced by none.
Disloyal guards
Would turn wolves and pards.
Man-eating tigers at daybreak
And at dusk blood-sucking long snake.
One may make merry in the Town of Silk*, I know,
But I would rather homeward go.
The road to Shu is harder than to climb to the sky,
I'd turn and westward look with long, long sigh.

* Chengdu, capital of Sichuan Province.

行 路 难

（三首其一）

金樽清酒斗十千①，
玉盘珍羞②直③万钱。
停杯投箸④不能食，
拔剑四顾心茫然。
欲渡黄河冰塞川，
将登太行雪满山。
闲来垂钓碧溪上，
忽复乘舟梦日边⑤。
行路难，
行路难，

① 斗十千：一斗值十千钱（即万钱），形容美酒价格昂贵。

② 珍羞：珍稀的菜肴。羞，同"馐"，美食。

③ 直：通"值"，价值。

④ 箸（zhù）：筷子。

⑤ 闲来垂钓碧溪上，忽复乘舟梦日边：表示诗人自己仍对从政抱有期待。这两句暗用典故：姜太公吕尚曾在渭水的磻溪上钓鱼，得遇周文王，助周灭商；伊尹曾梦见自己乘船从日月旁边经过，后被商汤聘请，助商灭夏。

《行路难》共三首，大约是李白第一次离开长安时写的，这是其中的第一首。如果说《蜀道难》是借山川险阻来写人生道路的艰难，那么《行路难》就是借历史人物的遭遇来抒发宣泄自己的苦闷。开头两句引用了曹植的"美酒斗十千"，说明自己是用黄金买醉，一如曹植的郁郁不得志。接着两句引用了鲍照《拟行路难》的"对案不能食，拔剑击柱长叹息"，反映自己内心的矛盾，这是第一层波澜。接下去又从地理上写到大河冰

Hard Is the Way of the World

(I)

Pure wine in golden cup costs ten thousand coppers, good!
Choice dish in a jade plate is worth as much, nice food!
Pushing aside my cup and chopsticks, I can't eat;
Drawing my sword and looking round, I stamp my feet.
I can't cross Yellow River: ice has stopped its flow;
I can't climb Mount Taihang: the sky is blind with snow.
I can but poise a fishing pole beside a stream
Or set sail for the sun like a sage in a dream.
Hard is the way,
Hard is the way.

冻、太行雪封,寸步难行,诗人不得不做退隐的打算,于是又引用了姜尚80岁钓鱼的典故,这是第二层波澜。下一句再引用伊尹梦见乘舟绕过日边,后来成了商代丞相的故事,自己的情绪也转为高昂,这是第三层波澜。最后,诗人摆脱了歧路彷徨的苦闷,发出了乘长风破万里浪,横渡沧海到达理想的彼岸的呼声。这样一波三折,表现了李白浪漫主义的乐观精神。

多歧路,

今安在?

长风破浪①会有时,

直挂云帆②济沧海。

① 长风破浪：引喻为实现政治理想。

② 云帆：高悬的船帆。船在海里航行，天水相接，船帆好似在云雾之中忽隐忽现。

Don't go astray!
Whither today?
A time will come to ride the wind and cleave the waves,
I'll set my cloud-white sail and cross the sea which raves.

行 路 难

(三首其二)

大道如青天,

我独不得出。

羞逐长安社①中儿,

赤鸡白狗赌梨栗。

弹剑②作歌奏苦声,

曳裾王门不称情。

淮阴市井笑韩信,

汉朝公卿忌贾生③。

① 社:古时二十五家为一社。

② 弹剑:战国时,齐公子孟尝君门下食客冯谖曾屡次弹剑作歌,以抒发内心抑郁不满之情。

③ 贾生:汉初洛阳贾谊,曾上书汉文帝,劝其改制兴礼,但却受到当时朝臣反对。

　　李白是一个很有才华的诗人,但他做不了一个政客。这首诗一开头陡起壁立,让胸中的万千感慨喷涌而出,也为下文埋下伏笔。原来诗人在政局中陷入困顿,明明大道通天,唯独自己却找不到出路,市井中斗鸡赌狗的泼皮,尚能谋得一官半职。其实诗人倒不是摸不到门路,而是不屑如此,他声明自己羞于与社中小儿为伍。至于达官贵人,又并不把他当一回事,使他像冯谖一样感到不能忍受。一般社会上的人对他嘲笑、

Hard Is the Way of the World
(II)

The way is broad like the blue sky,

But no way out before my eye.

I am ashamed to follow those who have no guts,

Gambling on fighting cocks and dogs for pears and nuts.

Feng would go homeward way, having no fish to eat;

Zhou did not think to bow to noblemen was meet.

General Han was mocked in the marketplace;

The brilliant scholar Jia was banished in disgrace.

轻视,当权者则忌妒、加以打击。"弹剑作歌奏苦声,曳裾王门不称情。淮阴市井笑韩信,汉朝公卿忌贾生。"是写他的不得志。诗人追求的是理想的君臣关系,即君明臣贤。他深情歌颂当初燕国君臣的互相尊重和信任。而当权阶级日渐昏庸腐朽,所以诗人发出了愤怒而又无奈的抗议:行路难,归去来!

君不见,
昔时燕家重郭隗,
拥篲①折节无嫌猜。
剧辛乐毅感恩分,
输肝剖胆效英才。
昭王白骨萦蔓草,
谁人更扫黄金台?
行路难,
归去来②!

① 拥篲:燕昭王亲自扫路,为防灰尘飞扬,用衣袖挡帚,以礼迎贤士邹衍。

② 归去来:指隐居。语出东晋陶渊明《归去来辞》。

Have you not heard of King of Yan in days gone by,
Who venerated talents and built Terrace high
On which he offered gold to gifted men
And stooped low and swept the floor to welcome them?
Grateful, Ju Xin and Yue Yi came then
And served him heart and soul, both full of stratagem.
The King's bones were now buried, who would sweep the floor
Of the Gold Terrace any more?
Hard is the way.
Go back without delay!

行 路 难

（三首其三）

有耳莫洗颍川水，
有口莫食首阳蕨①。
含光混世贵无名②，
何用孤高比云月？
吾观自古贤达人，
功成不退皆殒身。
子胥③既弃吴江上，
屈原终投湘水滨。
陆机④雄才岂自保？
李斯⑤税驾苦不早。

① 有口莫食首阳蕨：反用伯夷、叔齐典故。《史记·伯夷列传》："武王已平殷乱，天下宗周，而伯夷、叔齐耻之，义不食周粟，隐于首阳山，采薇而食之……遂饿死于首阳山。"《索引》："薇，蕨也。"按薇、蕨本二草，前人误以为一。

② 含光混世贵无名：言不露锋芒，随世俯仰之意。贵无名，以无名为贵。

③ 子胥：伍子胥，春秋末期吴国大夫。

④ 陆机：西晋文学家。《晋书·陆机传》载：陆机因宦人诬陷而被杀害于军中，临终叹曰："华亭鹤唳，岂可复闻乎？"

⑤ 李斯：秦国统一六国的大功臣，任秦朝丞相，后被杀。

　　这应是诗人离京时，宽慰自己之作。做人像许由一般孤傲，像伯夷叔齐一样清高，自诩唯有云月可比有什么用呢，做人还须"含光混世"、不务虚名。这既是诗人在长安期间得到的经验，也是对时局无奈的喟叹，因为他还未真正出世。诗人先后用伍子胥、屈原、陆机和李斯的事例，说明成功后贪恋名位不肯退隐的都殒丧了自己的性命。诗人或许是觉得，反正最后都要出世，又何必在乎早晚呢。

Hard Is the Way of the World
(III)

Don't wash your ears on hearing something you dislike

Nor die of hunger like famous hermits on the Pike!

Living without high fame among the motley crowd,

Why should one be as lofty as the moon or cloud?

Of ancient talents who failed to retire, there's none

But came to tragic ending after glory's won.

The head of General Wu was hung o'er city gate;

In the river was drowned the Poet Laureate.

The highly talented scholar wished in vain

To preserve his life to hear the cry of the crane.

华亭鹤唳讵可闻?
上蔡苍鹰何足道①?
君不见,
吴中张翰称达生,
秋风忽忆江东行②。
且乐生前一杯酒,
何须身后千载名?

① 华亭鹤唳讵可闻?上蔡苍鹰何足道?:用李斯典故。《史记·李斯列传》:"二世二年七月,具斯五刑,论腰斩咸阳市。斯出狱,与其中子俱执,顾谓其中子曰:'吾欲与若复牵黄犬俱出上蔡东门逐狡兔,岂可得乎!'"《太平御览》卷九二六:《史记》曰:"李斯临刑,思牵黄犬、臂苍鹰,出上蔡门,不可得矣。"

② 秋风忽忆江东行:用张翰典故。《晋书·张翰传》:"张翰,字季鹰,吴郡吴人也。……为大司马东曹掾。……因见秋风起,乃思吴中菰菜、莼羹、鲈鱼脍,曰:'人生贵得适志,何能羁宦数千里,以要名爵乎?'遂命驾而归。……或谓之曰:'卿乃纵适一时,独不为身后名邪?'答曰:'使我有身后名,不如即时一杯酒。'时人贵其旷达。"

Minister Li regretted not to have retired
To hunt with falcon gray as he had long desired.
Have you not heard of Zhang Han who resigned, carefree,
To go home to eat his perch with high glee?
Enjoy a cup of wine while you're alive!
Do not care if your fame will not survive!

送友人入蜀

见说蚕丛路①,
崎岖不易行。
山从人面起,
云傍马头生②。
芳树笼秦栈③,
春流④绕蜀城。
升沉⑤应已定,
不必问君平⑥。

① 蚕丛路:指入蜀的道路。蚕丛:蜀国的开国君王。

② 云傍马头生:云气依傍着马头而上升翻涌。

③ 秦栈:由秦(今陕西省)入蜀的栈道。

④ 春流:春江水涨,江水奔流。也可以指流经成都的郫江、流江。

⑤ 升沉:进退沉浮,即人在世间的境遇和命运。

⑥ 君平:西汉严遵,字君平,隐居不仕,曾在成都以卖卜为生。

这首诗是天宝二年(743)李白在长安送友人入蜀时所作,是一首以描绘蜀道山川的奇美而著称的抒情诗。开篇不同于《蜀道难》,而是语重心长,娓娓道来,欲语还休,情感真挚而诚恳。"山从人面起,云傍马头生",生动地再现了蜀道崎岖狭窄,境界飞逸奇美,韵味十足。"笼"字是为诸多评家所称道的"诗眼",非常传神,不是单纯写景,更是对上一联的呼应,很有表现力地描绘了蜀道的奇伟瑰丽,山岩的鬼斧神工。下句接合更妙,对仗工整,字字珠玑,带给读者强烈的色彩感。最后,诗人交代了他认为最重要也是一开始他就想说的,借用君平的典故,婉转地启发他的朋友不要沉迷于功名利禄之中,谆谆善诱,与开篇的欲语还休相呼应,情谊深挚,语短情长,又不乏对自身身世的感慨。

To a Friend Departing for Shu*

Rugg'd is the road, I hear,
Built by the pioneer.
In front steep mountains rise;
Beside the steed cloud flies.
O'er plank-way trees hang down;
Spring water girds the town.
Decid'd our rise and fall,
Do not bother at all!

* Present-day Sichuan Province.

春夜洛城①闻笛

① 洛城：即洛阳城，在今河南省洛阳市。

谁家玉笛②暗飞声？
散入东风满洛城。
此夜曲中闻《折柳》③，
何人不起故园情④？

② 玉笛：由玉制成或装饰的笛子。

③ 折柳：即《折杨柳》笛曲，乐府"鼓角横吹曲"调名，其内容多写离情别绪。而"折柳"又暗含古时人们临别时折柳相赠的一种习俗。柳，暗指"留"。

④ 故园情：思乡之情。故园，故乡。

　　这首诗可能是公元734年（一说735年）春天，李白寄居洛阳时写的。他在长安晋谒王公大人，一无所得。离开长安后，经过开封、商丘，流寓洛阳。在一个春天的暗夜里，他忽然听到幽怨的笛声，在夜深人静之际，随风吹入千家万户。唐代亲友分离之时，有折柳赠别的习俗。诗人一听到折柳曲，自然会产生思乡之情，这也流露了他的失意之感。如果说《静夜思》是见月思乡的话，这首诗就是闻笛思归了。

Hearing a Bamboo Flute on a Spring Night in Luoyang*

From whose house comes the voice of flute of jade unseen?
It fills the town of Luoyang, spread by wind of spring.
Tonight I hear the farewell song of *Willows Green*.
To whom the tune will not nostalgic feeling bring?

---

* The eastern capital during the Tang Dynasty.

塞下曲

(六首其一)

五月天山^①雪,

无花只有寒。

笛中闻《折柳》,

春色未曾看。

晓战随金鼓^②,

宵眠抱玉鞍。

愿将腰下剑,

直为斩楼兰。

① 天山:指祁连山。

② 金鼓:指锣,进军时击鼓,退军时鸣金。

    李白所作《塞下曲》共六首,此为其第一首。五月,在中原本是盛夏时节,李白所写五月在塞下,在天山,地域的差异带来的是所见所感的迥然有别。天山孤拔,终年积雪。同一季节景物上的巨大反差,在诗人的笔下并未显得波澜壮阔,只是淡淡地道出"无花只有寒",透着一丝苍凉。因为在边疆,将士们对苦寒习以为常,这里看不到春天,只能从笛曲之中,去感受,去回忆,何况又是《折柳》这样的"天涯人断肠"之曲,极力烘托渲染苍凉肃杀的气氛。后四句则是对军营生活的反映,以及对戍边将士们人人奋勇、争为功先的情感流露。朝,闻鼓搏战;暮,枕鞍而眠,极写军旅生活的紧张。尾联用了西汉傅介子的故事,借此表达了边塞将士的爱国激情。全篇苍凉雄浑,意境天成,是别具一格的边塞佳作。

Frontier Song

(I)

In summer sky-high mountains white with snow,
In bitter cold no fragrant flowers blow.
Songs on the flute are heard of *Willows Green*,
But nowhere is the vernal color seen.
From dawn till dusk to beats of drum they fight;
With saddle in their arms they rest at night.
From scabbard at my waist I'd draw my sword
To kill the chieftain of the Turki horde.

关山月[1]

[1] 关山月:乐府旧题,属横吹曲辞,多抒离别哀伤之情。

明月出天山,

苍茫云海间。

长风几万里,

吹度玉门关[2]。

汉下[3]白登道,

胡[4]窥[5]青海湾。

由来[6]征战地,

不见有人还。

戍客[7]望边色,

思归多苦颜。

高楼[8]当此夜,

叹息未应闲。

[2] 玉门关:故址在今甘肃敦煌西北,旧时通向西域的交通要塞。

[3] 下:指出兵。

[4] 胡:指吐蕃。

[5] 窥:觊觎,有所企图,窥伺,侵扰。

[6] 由来:自古以来。

[7] 戍客:戍守边疆的战士。

[8] 高楼:古诗中多以高楼指闺阁,这里理解为戍边兵士的妻子。

《关山月》是乐府旧题,作品很多,但都不如李白这首雄浑壮阔。前四句写驻扎在玉门关外的士兵,看见明月从天山上出来,徘徊在云海间,又经风吹万里,照到玉门关外,这是一幅动的图画。中四句的"白登"和"青海湾"分别是汉唐时代的战场,战士都是有去无返,可见诗人同情他们,景语也是情语。后四句写士兵思家,不说他们思念妻子,反说妻子思念他们,可见相互体贴感情之深。

The Moon over the Mountain Pass

From Heaven's Peak the moon rises bright,
Over a boundless sea of cloud.
Winds blow for miles with main and might
Past the Jade Gate which stands so proud.
Our warriors march down the frontier
While Tartars peer across Blue Bays.
From the battlefield outstretched here,
None have come back since olden days.
Guards watch the scene of borderland,
Thinking of home, with wistful eyes.
Tonight upstairs their wives would stand,
Looking afar with longing sighs.

乌夜啼[①]

[①] 乌夜啼：乐府旧题，多写男女离别相思之苦。

黄云城边乌欲栖，
归飞哑哑[②]枝上啼。
机中织锦[③]秦川女[④]，
碧纱如烟[⑤]隔窗语。
停梭[⑥]怅然忆远人，
独宿孤房泪如雨。

[②] 哑哑：乌鸦啼叫声。

[③] 机中织锦：一作"闺中织妇"。

[④] 秦川女：指晋朝苏蕙。《晋书·列女传》载，窦滔妻苏氏，始平人，名蕙，字若兰，善属文。窦滔原本是秦川刺史，后被苻坚徙流沙。苏蕙把思念织成回文璇玑图，题诗二百余，计八百余言，纵横反复皆成章句。泛指织锦女子。

[⑤] 碧纱如烟：指黄昏映着碧绿的窗纱朦胧似烟。

[⑥] 梭：织布用的织梭。形状似船，两头尖尖。远人，指遥远在外的丈夫。

许渊冲译李白诗选

这是一首离别相思之作，在主人公的塑造上，郑愁予的《错误》采用了同样的写作手法。乌鸦向来代表衰败荒凉，而黄昏时候，乌鸦尚且归巢，不能不让人"忧从中来"。首句就奠定了全诗的哀伤基调。诗人并未给出一个完整的等待征夫归来的女子的形象。我们只能推测"那等在季节里的容颜如莲花的开落"；我们也可以推测"足音不响，三月的春帷不揭"。但有一点是肯定的，窗后的女子的心，是"小小的窗扉紧掩"。透过纱窗，她的低语依稀可辨，织梭一停，一场泪雨。不由得使人怜惜感叹，可惜"我不是归人，是个过客"。

The Crows Crying at Night

'Neath yellow clouds the crows fly home by city wall,

They caw amid the leaves in treetops at night-fall.

The wife of Western Plain weaves brocade at her loom,

Behind the misty screen she murmurs — but to whom?

She stops her shuttle, thinking of him far away,

And weeps, so lonely in her bower night and day.

春　思

燕①草如碧丝，
秦②桑低绿枝。
当君③怀归日，
是妾④断肠时。
春风不相识，
何事入罗帏⑤?

① 燕：今河北省北部一带，此处泛指北疆地区，征夫所在之处。
② 秦：今陕西省一带，此指思妇所在之地。
③ 君：指征夫。
④ 妾：古代妇女自称。这里是思妇自指。
⑤ 罗帏：丝织的帷帐。

　　《春思》是李白描写妻子思念丈夫的一首小诗。仲春时节，桑叶繁茂，独处秦地的妻子见景生情，终日盼望驻扎在北方边境的丈夫早日归来，料想他看到碧丝般的春草，也会萌生对妻子的怀念。燕北地寒，春草生迟。当秦地柔桑低绿枝时，燕草方生，丈夫刚萌怀归之意，妻子思夫已经很久了。忽然春风吹开罗帐，妻子喜出望外以为丈夫回来，不料欢喜成空，于是转喜为悲，反而责怪春风不该闯入房中。这种想象中的责备之词，活画出了妻子思念丈夫的深情。

A Faithful Wife Longing for Her Husband in Spring

Your Northern grass must be like green silk thread;
Our Western mulberries have bent their head.
When your thoughts begin to turn homeward way,
My heart has long been breaking night and day.
To the intruding vernal wind I say:
"How dare you part the curtain of my bed!"

三五七言[①]

[①] 三五七言：一种诗歌体式，全诗三言、五言、七言各两句，因而得名。

秋风清，

秋月明。

落叶聚还散，

寒鸦栖复惊。

相思相见知何日？

此时此夜难为情！

　　《三五七言》写的是秋思。前二句每句三字，点明时间是个月白风清的秋夜。中二句每句五字，看得出地点是在树下，满地落叶堆积，被秋风吹到一起，又吹散了；树上的乌鸦感到秋凉，已经栖息，却被秋风秋月惊醒，象征着离散的情人不能入眠。后二句每句七字，写不能入眠的女子思念情人，何时能再见呢？如何度过这冷冷清清、孤孤单单的漫漫长夜呢？这种相思之情真是剪不断，理还乱，别是一般滋味在心头。《三五七言》的句型前短后长，也象征着秋思和秋夜一样越来越深。

Yearning

Fresh autumn breeze,
Bright autumn moon.
Fallen leaves gather and scatter around the trees;
Cold-stricken crows soon fall asleep and wake as soon.
I long for you. When can I see your longing look?
How can I bear this lonely night, this lonely nook?

怨　情

美人卷珠帘①，
深坐②颦③蛾眉④。
但看泪痕湿，
不知心恨谁。

① 卷珠帘：指卷起帷帘望向窗外。
② 深坐：长久的坐。
③ 颦（pín）：皱眉。
④ 蛾眉：蚕蛾触须弯而细长，因此以此借称女子之眉。

在中国古代的爱情诗中，写怨情的居多，李白这首五言绝句就是一个例子。如果说《春思》写了女性的内心，这首小诗却只写了美人的外形。第一句写她卷帘，可见有所期待；第二句写她皱眉，可见期待成空；第三句写泪痕，可见她由怨而哭；第四句并不点破她怨谁，是"忽见陌头杨柳色，悔教夫婿觅封侯"呢？还是"感此伤妾心，坐愁红颜老"呢？作者给读者留下了想象的空间，使人觉得语短情长。

Waiting in Vain

A lady fair uprolls the screen,

With eyebrows knit she waits in vain.

Wet stains of tears can still be seen.

Who, heartless, has caused her the pain?

玉阶怨[1]

[1] 玉阶怨：乐府古题，是专写"宫怨"的曲题。

玉阶生白露，
夜久侵罗袜[2]。
却下[3]水晶帘，
玲珑望秋月。

[2] 罗袜：丝织的袜子。

[3] 却下：回房放下。却：还。

如果说《怨情》通过写美人的外形来揭露内心的感情，那么《玉阶怨》却连外形都没有写，只是通过动作来暗示怨情。第一句"起"，"玉阶"表明地点是在宫内，"生白露"表明时间是在深夜。第二句"承"，"罗袜"表明宫女的身份，"侵罗袜"说明伫立时间已久。第三句"转"，"下水晶帘"表明失望。第四句"合"，"玲珑望月"却又表示还不死心，仿佛也要把一片痴情托付给明月，飞到所思念的人身边去。这样"起承转合"，使人从动作中看到宫女的内心，是不言怨而怨自见的写法。

Waiting in Vain on Marble Steps

The marble steps with dew turn cold,
Silk soles are wet when night grows old.
She comes in, lowers crystal screen,
Still gazing at the moon serene.

长门怨[1]

(二首其一)

[1] 长门怨：古乐府诗题。

天回北斗[2]挂西楼，
金屋无人萤火流。
月光欲到长门殿，
别作深宫一段愁。

[2] 天回北斗：北斗七星。古人往往据初昏时斗柄所指方向以定季节。《鹖冠子·环流》："斗柄东指，天下皆春；斗柄南指，天下皆夏；斗柄西指，天下皆秋；斗柄北指，天下皆冬。"此句指此时节为秋。

　　长门宫是汉武帝的陈皇后居住的冷宫。陈皇后小名阿娇，汉武帝小时曾说："若得阿娇为妇，当作金屋贮之。"所以后世就有"金屋藏娇"之说。不料阿娇从金屋打入了冷宫，长门怨也就变成了冷宫怨。这一首写景不写人，金屋景色凄清，天上只有北斗横斜，地上只见萤火流动，明月洒下幽光，照着长门深宫，显得愁上加愁，分外凄凉。

Sorrow of the Long Gate Palace*

(I)

The plough has turned around and hangs o'er Western Tower,
None but the fireflies sail the gloom of Golden Bower.
The lonely moon which peeps in Palace of Long Gate
Will shed more sorrow on the dweller desolate.

---

* The Long Gate Palace was the dwelling of a disfavored queen of the Han Dynasty.

长 门 怨

（二首其二）

桂殿[①]长愁不记春，　　　　　　① 桂殿：指长门殿。
黄金四屋[②]起秋尘。　　　　　　② 四屋：四壁。
夜悬明镜[③]青天上，　　　　　　③ 明镜：指月亮。
独照长门宫里人。

　　这首着重写情，桂殿似乎成了秋天的一统天下，冷宫似乎没有见过春天，金屋的灰尘也没人打扫，留下了永恒的秋色。夜里，秋月犹如明镜照着冷宫里孤独的陈皇后，仿佛月宫里冷冷清清的嫦娥也向她洒下了同情之泪。如果说《玉阶怨》写的是宫女之怨，那《长门怨》写的就是后妃之怨了。

Sorrow of the Long Gate Palace

(II)

Does Laurel Bower where grief reigns remember spring?
On the four golden walls the dusts of autumn cling.
The night holds up a mirror bright in azure sky
To show the fair on earth as lonely as on high.

子夜吴歌

（春歌）

秦地[1]罗敷女[2]，
采桑绿水边。
素手青条上，
红妆白日鲜。
蚕饥妾[3]欲去，
五马莫留连！

[1] 秦地：现今陕西省关中地区。
[2] 罗敷(fū)女：乐府诗《陌上桑》有"日出东南隅，照我秦氏楼。秦氏有好女，自言名罗敷。罗敷善蚕桑，采桑城南隅"的诗句。
[3] 妾：古代女子用以自称的谦词。

《子夜吴歌》共四首，分咏春、夏、秋、冬四季。六朝乐府有《子夜四时歌》，诗人依前人所创做了革新，将诗体由四句加为六句，手法也更胜一筹。此一首为春歌，这首诗吟咏罗敷女的故事，赞扬她不为富贵动心，不仅有美貌，更有美丽的心灵，她的勤劳品质在"蚕饥妾欲去，五马莫留连"一句中得到了很好的阐述。《汉官仪》："四马载车，此常礼也，惟太守出，则增一马。"故称五马，这里指达官贵人。

Ballads of Four Seasons

(Spring)

The lovely Lo Fo* of the western land

Plucks mulberry leaves by the waterside.

Across the green boughs stretches out her white hand;

In golden sunshine her rosy robe is dyed.

"My silkworms are hungry, I cannot stay.

Tarry not with your five-horse cab, I pray."

---

* Lo Fo and below-mentioned Xi Shi were beautiful ladies.

子夜吴歌

（夏歌）

镜湖①三百里，
菡萏②发荷花。
五月西施采，
人看隘若耶③。
回舟不待月，
归去越王④家！

① 镜湖：位于今浙江省绍兴市东南。

② 菡(hàn)萏(dàn)：荷花的别称。古人将未开的荷花称为"菡萏"，即花苞。

③ 若耶(yē)：若耶溪，今浙江省绍兴市境内。溪边原有浣纱石古迹，相传西施曾在此浣纱，又名"浣纱溪"。

④ 越王：即越王勾践。

《夏歌》写的是西施，她具有更深一层的美丽。她的美就像是湖中竞开的荷花，明明镜湖三百里，却因她太美，以致前来看她的人群使若耶都变得狭隘。然而西施的命运却是如此令人感慨，同样是由于她倾国倾城的美，"回舟不待月，归去越王家"。

Ballads of Four Seasons

(Summer)

On Mirror Lake outspread for miles and miles,
The lotus lilies in full blossom teem.
In fifth moon Xi Shi gathers them with smiles,
Watchers o'erwhelm the bank of Yoya Stream.
Her boat turns back without waiting moonrise
To royal house amid amorous sighs.

子夜吴歌

（秋歌）

长安一片月，

万户捣衣声。

秋风吹不尽，

总是玉关①情。

何日平胡虏②？

良人③罢远征！

① 玉关：玉门关，故址在今甘肃省敦煌市西北，此处代指良人戍边之地。

② 平胡虏：平定侵扰边境的敌人。

③ 良人：古时妇女称呼丈夫"良人"。

这首写的是妻子对边防士兵的怀念，开拓了吴歌的境界。诗从客观的写景入手，首先展现出月下万户捣衣的情景。捣衣是将衣料放在石砧上用木杵捶打，使之柔软，便于裁缝，制成衣服可以寄去边关。诗人听到风吹捣衣之声，仿佛是捣衣女对驻守玉门关外的丈夫的思念之情。西风吹不尽，思念之情也就不尽。最后，诗人设身处地为捣衣女着想，希望早日战胜边境的敌人，罢战之后，丈夫可以回到家乡。这样剥茧抽丝，先景后情，由远及近，由外到内，丝越抽越细，情越转越深，无怪乎王夫之说"前四句是天壤间生成好句，被太白拾得"了。

Ballads of Four Seasons

(Autumn)

Moonlight is spread all o'er the capital,
The sound of beating clothes far and near
Is brought by autumn wind which can't blow all
The longings away for far-off frontier.
When can we vanquish the barbarian foe
So that our men no longer into battle go?

子夜吴歌

（冬歌）

明朝驿使①发，
一夜絮征袍。
素手②抽针冷，
那堪把剪刀！
裁缝寄远道，
几日到临洮③？

① 驿使：驿站里负责传送文书、物件的人；驿：驿站、驿管。

② 素手：指妇女白皙的双手。

③ 临洮：在今甘肃省定西市，此泛指边地。

《冬歌》采用的是另一种写法。没有景物描写，代以叙事。事件被安排在一个有意味的时刻——传送征衣的驿使即将出发的前夜，大大增强了此诗的情节性和戏剧味。此诗的中心围绕着一个矛盾展开，天气寒冷，"素手抽针冷，那堪把剪刀"，而驿使明天就要出发，时间太紧迫。由此看来，诗中女子是想多些时间将征袍细细做来的，但又想到"裁缝寄远道，几日到临洮"，又恨不得马上完成，好让驿使赶紧出发。这种矛盾，塑造出一个活生生的思妇形象，成功表达了诗歌的主题。

Ballads of Four Seasons

(Winter)

The courier will depart next day, she's told,

She sews a warrior's gown all night.

Her fingers feel the needle cold.

How can she hold the scissors tight?

The work is done, she sends it far away.

When will it reach the town where warriors stay?

将①进酒

① 将(qiāng)：请、愿。

君不见黄河之水天上来，
奔流到海不复回！
君不见高堂②明镜悲白发，
朝如青丝暮成雪！
人生得意须尽欢，
莫使金樽空对月。
天生我材必有用，
千金散尽还复来。
烹羊宰牛且为乐，
会须一饮三百杯。

② 高堂：高大的厅堂上。

《将进酒》是李白奉诏上长安，又被"赐金还山"后的作品。他在洛阳遇到两位朋友，三人开怀畅饮，就写下了这首劝酒诗。开始他写黄金岁月犹如黄河流水一样一去不返，满头青丝已有白发，而自己却壮志未酬，不禁悲从中来。但是悲中有壮，因为道路虽然坎坷，失望还没变成绝望，所以发出了"天生我材必有用"的呼声。但一想到荣华富贵转

Invitation to Wine

Do you not see the Yellow River come from the sky,

Rushing into the sea and ne'er come back?

Do you not see the mirrors bright in chambers high

Grieve o'er your snow-white hair though once it was silk-black?

When hopes are won, oh! Drink your fill in high delight,

And never leave your wine cup empty in moonlight!

Heaven has made us talents, we're not made in vain.

A thousand gold coins spent, more will turn up again.

Kill a cow, cook a sheep and let us merry be,

And drink three hundred cupfuls of wine in high glee!

眼消逝,古代圣贤也不得志,如才华绝代的曹植都被闲置不用,只靠饮酒作乐来打发日子。自己也只好学他那样,卖马换酒,尽情一醉,把自己积郁千年的忧愁设法一扫而光。诗中忽悲忽乐,忽乐忽悲,悲中有乐,乐中有悲,这样波澜起伏,曲折多姿,反映了李白的矛盾心理,也反映了唐代社会光明与阴暗交错、光明还掩盖着黑暗的现实。

岑夫子,
丹丘生①,
将进酒,
杯莫停。
与君歌一曲,
请君为我侧耳听。
钟鼓②馔玉③不足贵,
但愿长醉不复醒。
古来圣贤皆寂寞,
惟有饮者留其名。
陈王④昔时宴平乐,
斗酒十千恣⑤欢谑。
主人何为言少钱,
径须沽⑥取对君酌。
五花马, 千金裘,
呼儿将出换美酒,
与尔同销万古愁。

① 岑(cén)夫子, 丹丘生: 指岑勋和元丹丘, 二人均为李白的好友。

② 钟鼓: 富贵人家宴会时奏乐使用的乐器。
③ 馔玉: 形容如玉石一样精美的食物。

④ 陈王: 指陈思王曹植。
⑤ 恣: 纵情任意、无拘无束。

⑥ 沽: 通"酤", 买或卖, 这里指买。

Dear friends of mine,

Cheer up, cheer up!

I invite you to wine.

Do not put down your cup!

I will sing you a song, please hear,

O hear! Lend me a willing ear!

What difference will rare and costly dishes make?

I only want to get drunk and never to wake.

How many great men were forgotten through the ages?

But great drinkers are more famous than sober sages.

The Prince of Poets feast'd in his palace at will,

Drank wine at ten thousand a cask and laughed his fill.

A host should not complain of money he is short,

To drink with you I will sell things of any sort.

My fur coat worth a thousand coins of gold

And my flower-dappled horse may be sold

To buy good wine that we may drown the woe age-old.

赠孟浩然

吾爱孟夫子[①],
风流[②]天下闻。
红颜弃轩冕,
白首卧松云。
醉月频中圣[③],
迷花不事君[④]。
高山[⑤]安可仰?
徒此揖清芬。

① 孟夫子:指孟浩然。夫子,一般的尊称。
② 风流:古人以风流赞美文人,主要是指有文采,善词章,风度潇洒,不钻营苟且等。
③ 中圣:"中圣人"的简称,即醉酒。中:读去声,动词,"中暑"之"中",此为饮清酒而醉,故曰中圣。
④ 事君:侍奉皇帝。
⑤ 高山:形容孟浩然品格高尚,令人敬仰。另有《经·小雅·车舝》:"高山仰止,景行行止"。

  孟浩然是比李白年长12岁的诗人,这首诗大约是公元739年写的。第一联开门见山,写孟浩然潇洒的风度和不凡的才华。第二联说他年轻时不羡慕车马官服,后来又热爱松风白云,从反面说到正面。第三联却从正面到反面,说他宁可做月下饮酒的圣人,不做侍奉君王的大臣。最后用《诗经》中"高山仰止"的形象,把自己的爱慕具体化。这是一首用飘逸风格来写飘逸诗人、不为格律所拘的五言律诗。

To Meng Haoran

Dear Master Meng, I hail you from the heart,
Of your high value all the world is proud.
Red-cheek'd, from cap to cab you kept apart;
White-haired, you lie beneath the pine and cloud.
Drunken with wine as oft as with moonlight,
You love the blooms too much to serve the crown.
Of lofty mountain how to reach the height?
We can but breathe your fragrance the wind brings down.

夜泊牛渚怀古

牛渚①西江②夜,
青天无片云。
登舟望秋月,
空忆谢将军③。
余亦能高咏,
斯人④不可闻。
明朝挂帆席,
枫叶落纷纷。

① 牛渚：山名，在今安徽省马鞍山市西南。

② 西江：从南京以西到江西境内的一段长江，古代称西江。

③ 谢将军：东晋谢尚，今河南省周口市太康县人，官镇西将军。

④ 斯人：指谢尚。

牛渚在安徽马鞍山，山脚插入长江，就是著名的采石矶。李白月夜泊舟牛渚，不禁想起了晋朝镇守牛渚的谢将军，将军赞赏袁宏在船上朗诵的咏史诗，使袁宏声名大振。而李白和袁宏同病相怜，却没有人扶持。最后诗人又想象离开时的落叶秋色，用写景来衬托不遇知音的寂寞情怀。王夫之说这首诗是"不着一字，尽得风流"的典型。李白死后就葬在采石矶。

Thoughts on Old Time from a Night-Mooring near Cattle Hill

I moor near Cattle Hill at night
When there's no cloud to fleck the sky.
On deck I gaze at the moon so bright,
Thinking of General Xie* with a sigh.
I too can chant — to what avail?
None has like him a listening ear.
Tomorrow I shall hoist my sail,
'Mid fallen maple leaves I'll leave here.

---

* General Xie of the Jin Dynasty (265–420) praised a young poet who chanted his poem one moonlit night on the river by Cattle Hill (in present-day Anhui Province).

客中^①行

① 客中:指旅居他乡。

兰陵^②美酒郁金香,
玉碗^③盛来琥珀光。
但使^④主人能醉客^⑤,
不知何处是他乡。

② 兰陵:今山东省临沂市苍山县兰陵镇。
③ 玉碗:玉制的食具,亦泛指精美的碗。
④ 但使:只要。
⑤ 醉客:让客人喝醉酒;醉,使动用法。

    李白曾在开元年间移居东鲁,这首诗作于东鲁的兰陵,而称兰陵为"客中",因此当作于移居东鲁之前。兰陵虽是做客之地,但和美酒联系起来,就带有留恋的感情色彩;加上美酒是用郁金香加工浸制的,有醇浓的香味,盛在晶莹的玉碗里,看起来就像琥珀一般光艳。这样的美酒还有好客的主人作陪,所以诗人虽然身在客中,却乐而忘忧,不觉得是在他乡了。这首诗被法国女诗人戈谢译成法文,又被德国作曲家马勒编为《大地之歌》第三乐章,在全世界广为流传。

While Journeying

How flavorous is golden-tuliped Lanling* wine!
Filling my bowl of jade, in amber it will glow.
It is enough if you can make me drunk, host mine,
No more nostalgia in foreign land shall I know.

* In present-day Shandong Province.

陌上赠美人

骏马骄①行踏落花,
垂鞭直②拂五云车③。
美人一笑褰④珠箔,
遥指红楼⑤是妾家。

①骄:指高大健壮的骏马。
②直:特地,故意。
③五云车:传说中神仙的座驾。这里指华美的车驾。
④褰:提起,撩起。
⑤红楼:一作青楼。

芳草鲜美、落英缤纷的季节,骑着高大骏马的英姿勃发的男子,潇洒地走在路上,完全是一个"白马王子"的形象。五云车是传说中神仙乘的车,这样华丽的香车中乘坐的是怎样的女子呢?于是拍马上前,挥鞭拂车。纤纤玉手掀起珠帘,珠帘后是如花笑靥,指着不远的红楼道,那是我的家。这是一首爱情诗,诗的画面感很强,诗人绘声绘色地勾勒了一幅浪漫唯美的画面。

To a Fair Lady Encountered on the Road

I trample fallen flowers on a steed so proud,
And flick my whip at a cab of five-colored cloud.
The jewelled curtain drawn reveals a lady fair.
Smiling, she points to a mansion red, "My house is there."

登太白峰[①]

[①] 太白峰：太白山，又名太乙山、太一山。山峰极高，常有积雪。

西上太白[②]峰，
夕阳穷登攀。
太白与我语，
为我开天关[③]。
愿乘泠风[④]去，
直出浮云间。
举手可近月，
前行若无山。
一别武功[⑤]去，
何时复更还？

[②] 太白：指太白星，即金星。这里喻指仙人。

[③] 天关：古星名，又名天门。《晋书·天文志》："东方，角宿二星为天关，其间天门也，其内天庭也。故黄道经其中，七曜之所行也。"这里指想象中的天界门户。

[④] 泠（líng）风：和煦轻微之风。

[⑤] 武功：古代武功县。

李白于公元742年应诏入京时，踌躇满志。但是，由于朝廷昏庸，权贵排斥，他的政治抱负根本无法实现，这使他感到惆怅与苦闷。此诗即作于这个时期。即使是李白遍访名山求仙问道，在他的想象中，也应该是神仙主动搭话。因为他不被凡夫俗子所理解，只能想象具有更高深的思想意识的神仙来理解他、抚慰他。所以诗中太白星来同他攀谈，为他打开天门，而诗人自己也表示愿意随他同往仙境，从侧面显示了诗人仕途的失意和对现实的不满。正当诗人于想象中徜徉时，回头看见人间，此一别，何时还？一丝留恋，萦绕心间。

Ascending the Snow-White Peak*

Ascending from the west the Peak Snow-White,
Not till the sun goes down I reach its height.
The snow-white Morning Star tells me to wait
Until he opens the Celestial Gate.
I wish to ride cold wind and floating cloud
To touch the moon and dwarf all mountains proud.
But once I left behind the Western land,
Could I return to the summit where I stand?

---

* Or the Great White Mountain in Shaanxi Province.

登广武古战场怀古

秦鹿①奔野草,
逐之若飞蓬。
项王气盖世,
紫电明双瞳②。
呼吸③八千人,
横行起江东。
赤精斩白帝,
叱咤入关中。
两龙④不并跃,
五纬与天同。
楚灭无英图,
汉兴有成功。

① 秦鹿:出自"逐鹿"典故。《史记》:蒯通曰:"秦失其鹿,天下共逐之,于是高材捷足者先得焉。"张晏曰:"以鹿喻帝位也。"

② 双瞳:传说项羽眼球有两个瞳孔。《史记·项羽本纪》:"闻项羽亦重瞳子。"

③ 呼吸:一呼即来。

④ 两龙:指刘邦和项羽。

　　这是一首大气磅礴的诗,读来令人荡气回肠。前半部分概括从秦末到汉初的历史,但写得非常生动,人物描写各具特色,形象丰满,活灵活现。后半部分则是站在今者的角度去思考去想象,"拨乱属豪圣,俗儒安可通",拨乱反正、力挽狂澜从来都需要英雄豪杰,凡夫俗子能干些什么呢?结尾更是借阮籍讽刺庸俗的儒生无用,只会诋毁英雄。这首诗显示了作者对建功立业的向往,也从侧面反映了现实中诗人的处境。

Reflections on the Ancient Battlefield at Guangwu[*]

The Emperor of Qin had lost his deer[†],
And heroes chased it as thistle-down flies.
The Prince of Chu was brave without a peer,
With purple flashes in double-pupiled eyes.
He called eight thousand Southern youths to fight,
From eastern River shore they swept the foes.
The Duke of Han had killed the Serpent white,
And breaking through the Pass, his war cries rose.
Two rival Dragons reigned not at same time,
And five propitious stars appeared on high.
Chu perished for lack of ideal sublime;
The Duke expanded his realm beneath the sky.

---

[*] The battlefield in present-day Henan Province where Xiang Yu, Prince of Chu, fought against Liu Bang, Duke of Han, who won and became the first emperor of the Han Dynasty in 206 B.C.

[†] His throne.

按剑清八极^①,
归酣歌《大风》。
伊昔临广武,
连兵^②决雌雄。
分我一杯羹,
太皇乃汝翁。
战争有古迹,
壁垒颓层穹。
猛虎啸洞壑,
饥鹰鸣秋空。
翔云列晓阵,
杀气赫长虹。
拨乱属豪圣,
俗儒安可通?
沉湎呼竖子,
狂言非至公。
抚掌黄河曲,
嗤嗤阮嗣宗。

① 八极:指最边远的地方。

② 连兵:兵刃相连,正面交锋。

He cleared eight borders with the sword he did wield,
And came back drunk and sang *The Great Wind Song*[*].
His army once came to this battlefield,
And fought the Prince to see who was the strong.
His father, captured, would be boiled alive,
"My father's yours," he said, "in weal and woe."
Of ancient war few relics still survive,
The ramparts crumble to mounds high and low.
Fierce growling tigers fill the caves with dismay,
And hungry eagles cleave the autumn sky.
The morning clouds still make a battle array,
And war cries seem to pelt the rainbow on high.
To end disorder is the deed of sage.
Pedantic scholar[†], how dare you declare,
Drunken, the Duke was fellow of village?
You're mad and frenzy, unjust and unfair.
I clap my hands in view of this battleground,
And laugh away your ignorance profound.

---

[*] The first seven-charactered poem written by Liu Bang.

[†] Ruan Ji, scholar of the Jin Dynasty (265–420), who said on his visit to the battlefield at Guangwu that there was no hero in the world and a village fellow like Liu Bang had risen to fame.

南陵①别儿童入京

① 南陵:位于今安徽省芜湖市南陵县。

白酒新熟山中归,
黄鸡啄黍②秋正肥。
呼童烹鸡酌白酒,
儿女嬉笑牵人衣。
高歌取醉欲自慰,
起舞落日争光辉。
游说③万乘④苦不早,
著鞭跨马涉远道。
会稽愚妇轻买臣⑤,
余亦辞家西入秦。
仰天大笑出门去,
我辈岂是蓬蒿人⑥?

② 黍:古代专指一种子实叫黍子的一年生草本植物。

③ 游说:战国时,有才之人以口辩舌战打动诸侯,获取官位,称为游说。
④ 万乘(shèng):此处指君主、皇帝。周朝制度,天子地方千里,车万乘。后来称皇帝为万乘。
⑤ 买臣:朱买臣,西汉会稽郡吴(今江苏省苏州市境内)人。
⑥ 蓬蒿人:草野之人,即无官职的平民百姓。

公元742年,李白接到入京的诏书。他以为自己的政治理想终于得以实现,遂与儿女告别,并写下此诗。山中游玩归来,时值浅秋,仓满黍黄,肥鸡新酒,一派丰收景象,开篇为全诗的情感基调做了铺垫。接下来的四句,则表现力十足地渲染这股欢愉的氛围,"嬉笑""歌""醉""起舞",欢欣鼓舞之情溢于言表。"游说万乘苦不早,著鞭跨马涉远道"表现诗人高兴之余,又有些"恨晚",更巴不得马上踏上仕途,表达自己的政治主张。作者以晚年得志的朱买臣自比,以会稽愚妇讽刺轻视自己的世俗小人。末尾两句是诗人情感的宣泄,把诗人踌躇满志的形象表现得淋漓尽致。

Parting from My Children at Nanling* for the Capital

I come to hillside home when wine is newly brewed,
And yellow chicken feed on grains which autumn's strewed.
I call my lad to boil the fowl and pour the wine,
My children tug me by the sleeve, their faces shine.
I sing away to show my joy when wine is drunk;
I dance to vie in splendor with the sun half sunk.
Though it is late to offer service to the crown,
Still I will spur my horse on my way to renown.
The silly wife despised the talent not yet blest,
I'll leave my family and journey to the west.
Looking up at the sky, I laugh aloud and go.
Am I a man to crawl amid the brambles low?

* In present-day Anhui Province.

清平调①词

（三首其一）

① 清平调：唐大曲名，后用为词牌。

云想衣裳花想容，
春风拂槛②露华浓③。
若非群玉④山头见，
会⑤向瑶台⑥月下逢。

② 槛：栏杆。
③ 露华浓：牡丹花沾着晶莹的露珠更显得颜色艳丽。
④ 群玉：山名，中西王母所住之地。
⑤ 会：应。
⑥ 瑶台：亦指西王母所居宫殿。

《清平调词》是李白写杨贵妃的名篇。他把杨贵妃和牡丹花合在一起写，写花也是写人。第一句说：见云可以想到美人的衣裳，见花可以想到她的美貌；也可以说是把衣裳想象为云，把美貌想象为花。第二句的春风可以暗喻君王的恩宠，说牡丹花在晶莹的露水中更显得浓艳。接着，第三句把杨贵妃比作群玉山头的仙女，第四句又比作月中瑶台前的嫦娥，这都是从空间上把她比作天仙的。

The Beautiful Lady Yang[*]

(I)

Her face is seen in flower and her dress in cloud,
A beauty by the rails caressed by vernal breeze.
If not a Fairy Queen from Jade-Green Mountains proud,
She's Goddess of the Moon in Crystal Hall one sees.

---

[*] Lady Yang Yuhuan was the favorite concubine of Tang Emperor Xuanzong (reigned 725–768).

清平调词

（三首其二）

一枝红艳露凝香，
云雨巫山枉断肠。
借问汉宫谁得似？
可怜飞燕①倚新妆②。

① 飞燕：指西汉皇后赵飞燕。
② 妆：梳妆打扮。

  第二首第一句再把美人比花，不但写色，而且写香。然后从时间上来比，先比作楚襄王为之断肠的、朝为行云暮为雨的巫山神女，后比作汉成帝的宠妃，能做掌上舞的赵飞燕。不过飞燕倚仗新妆，杨妃却是天姿国色，这样借古喻今，又是抑古扬今了。

The Beautiful Lady Yang

(II)

She is a peony sweetened by dew impearled,

Far fairer than the Goddess* bringing showers in dreams.

Who could equal her in palace of ancient world?

Not e'en the newly-dressed "Flying Swallow"†, it seems.

---

* The legend said that the king of a Southern Kingdom dreamed of the Goddess of Wushan Mountains with whom he made love and who would come out in the morning in the form of a cloud and in the evening in the form of a shower.

† "Flying Swallow" was the favorite concubine of Han Emperor Chengdi (reigned 32–6 B.C.)

清平调词

（三首其三）

名花①倾国②两相欢，
长得③君王带笑看。
解释春风无限恨，
沉香亭北倚阑干。

① 名花：指牡丹花。
② 倾国：指杨贵妃。
③ 得：使。

第三首从仙境和古代回到现实中来，写倾国倾城的美人在沉香亭北倚栏赏花，使得君王百看不厌，解除了他的无限忧恨。语语浓艳，字字流芳，使美人名花融合为一，流传千古。

The Beautiful Lady Yang

(III)

The lady fair admires and is admired by the flower,
The sovereign would gaze upon her with a smile.
She leans on balustrade north of the Fragrant Bower,
The longing of spring wind she knows how to beguile.

忆东山①

（二首其一）

①东山：在今浙江省绍兴市上虞区西南，相传是谢安曾游宴的地方。山上有谢安所建的白云、明月二堂。

不向东山久，

蔷薇几度花②？

②花：此处为动词，意为开花。

白云还自散，

明月落谁家？

东山是东晋著名政治家谢安曾经隐居的地方。李白写这首诗的时候，大约正在长安。接到诏书入京之后，李白并没有得到谢安那样大展雄才的机会，反而由于放浪不羁，招致权贵的忌恨。他开始怀念以前的隐居了，他沉吟在流逝的时光中，感叹岁月蹉跎，他有些想离开了。诗中充满了何去何从的疑惑，透过这白云明月，诗人的情怀展露无遗。

The Eastern Hill[*]

(I)

Once more I come to Eastern Hill.

How many times has blown the rose?

White clouds gather and scatter still.

Where sinks the moon of yore? Who knows?

---

[*] Xie An, poet-governor of the 4th century, resided in the Eastern Hill where there was a Cave of Roses, and he built the Hall of White Cloud and the Hall of Bright Moon on top of the hill (in present-day Zhejiang Province).

乌栖曲[1]

[1] 乌栖曲：乐府《清商曲辞》西曲歌调名。

姑苏台上乌栖时，
吴王宫里醉西施。
吴歌楚舞[2]欢未毕，
青山欲衔半边日。
银箭金壶[3]漏水多，
起看秋月坠江波，
东方渐高[4]奈乐何！

[2] 吴歌楚舞：吴楚两国的歌舞。

[3] 银箭金壶：指刻漏，古时候的计时工具。

[4] 东方渐高(hào)：东方渐晓；高，同"皜"，白色，这里指晓色。

《乌栖曲》是乐府旧题，但李白写的却非情歌艳曲。开篇写得虽是奢靡之境，却极简练，寥寥数笔，就勾画出日落时分姑苏台上吴宫的轮廓和宫中美人醉态朦胧的剪影，且更具象征意义。乌鸦代表衰败，夕阳下昏暗的吴宫，没有一丝帝王将相该有的文治武功之象，使人联想到吴国正在走向没落。在这样的氛围中，却有不合时宜的豪歌痛饮，欢未毕而时已暮。滴漏声声，长夜消逝，欢乐难继，好梦不再。享乐者的夜未央之梦，也必将破碎。诡异的表象下是鲜明的对照，诗人揭示了贪图享受的统治者的内心，讽刺当权者荒淫无道、不问国政。

Crows Going Back to Their Nest

— Satire on the King of Wu*

O'er Royal Terrace when crows flew back to their nest,

The king in Royal Palace feast'd his mistress drunk.

The Southern maidens sang and danced without a rest

Till beak-like mountain-peaks would peck the sun half sunk.

The golden clepsydra could not stop water's flow,

O'er river waves the autumn moon was hanging low.

But wouldn't the king enjoy his fill in Eastern glow?

---

* The king of Wu held perpetual revelries with his favorite mistress Xi Shi in his Royal Palace in the 5th century B.C.

下终南山过斛斯山人宿置酒

暮从碧山①下，
山月随人归。
却顾所来径②，
苍苍横翠微③。
相携及田家，
童稚开荆扉④。
绿竹入幽径，
青萝拂行衣。
欢言得所憩，
美酒聊共挥。
长歌吟松风，
曲尽河星稀。
我醉君复乐，
陶然共忘机⑤。

① 碧山：指终南山。

② 所来径：下山的小路。

③ 翠微：青翠的山坡，此处亦指终南山。

④ 荆扉：荆条编扎的小门。

⑤ 忘机：忘记世俗、不谋虚名；机：世俗的心机。

终南山在长安以南，唐代有士人在山中隐居，斛斯山人就是其中一个。李白游终南山下来，月亮似乎也随着他下山了，小路仿佛融进了一片苍翠的山色中。"相携"指斛斯山人，如果说是指月，那倒别有风趣。诗人与山人欢聚畅谈，饮酒挥洒自如，其乐融融，两人都甘于恬淡，与世无争。全诗平平淡淡，随随便便，浑不着力，并无惊人之句，然而诗中充溢着的是大自然的纯朴之美和诗人的真率之情。

Descending Zhongnan Mountain*
and Meeting Husi the Hermit

At dusk I leave the hills behind,
The moon escorts me all the way.
Looking back, I see the path wind
Across the woods so green and grey.
We come to your cot hand in hand,
Your lad opens the gate for me.
Bamboos along the alley stand
And vines caress my cloak with glee.
I'm glad to talk and drink good wine
Together with my hermit friend.
We sing the songs of wind and pine,
And stars are set when singings end.
I'm drunk and you're merry and glad:
We both forget the world is sad.

---

* South of Chang'an, the Tang capital.

月下独酌

（四首其一）

花间一壶酒，
独酌无相亲[1]。　　　　　　① 无相亲：没有亲近的人。
举杯邀明月，
对影成三人。
月既不解饮，
影徒随我身。
暂伴月将[2]影，　　　　　　② 将：共，伴同。
行乐须及春。
我歌月徘徊，
我舞影零乱。
醒时同交欢[3]，　　　　　　③ 同交欢：一起欢乐。
醉后各分散。
永结无情游，　　　　　　　④ 相期邈云汉：约定在天上相见；
相期邈云汉[4]。　　　　　　　期：约会；邈：遥远；云汉：银
　　　　　　　　　　　　　　河，这里指仙境。

　　公元744年，李白对"珠玉买歌笑，糟糠养贤才"的长安生活不满，感到寂寞，就去花间饮酒，写下了这首名作。开始两句写他孤独，"举杯"两句显得旷达，"月既"两句又写孤独，"暂伴"两句又似旷达。前八句是起伏相间，一抑一扬。接着四句不但旷达，而且俊逸。最后两句把想

Drinking Alone under the Moon

(I)

Amid the flowers, from a pot of wine
I drink alone beneath the bright moonshine.
I raise my cup to invite the Moon who blends
Her light with my Shadow and we're three friends.
The Moon does not know how to drink her share;
In vain my Shadow follows me here and there.
Together with them for the time I stay
And make merry before spring's spent away.
I sing and the Moon lingers to hear my song;
My Shadow's a mess while I dance along.
Sober, we three remain cheerful and gay;
Drunken, we part and each may go his way.
Our friendship will outshine all earthly love,
Next time we'll meet beyond the stars above.

象引向高远，真是"飘然思不群"了。但孤独是现实，旷达是幻想。诗写得越旷达，越显得诗人孤独。不过幻想是对现实的否定和批判，所以旷达显示了积极的精神力量，造就了诗的美感。

把酒问月

青天有月来几时?
我今停杯一问之。
人攀明月不可得,
月行却与人相随。
皎如飞镜临丹阙①,
绿烟②灭尽清辉发。
但见宵从海上来,
宁知晓向云间没③?
白兔捣药秋复春,
嫦娥孤栖与谁邻?

① 丹阙:朱红色的宫殿。

② 绿烟:遮蔽月光的浓重云雾。

③ 没(mò):隐没。

　　这是一首咏月抒怀诗。酒酣之际,诗人抬头看到亘古不变的月亮,对宇宙的冥冥发出了饱含哲理的疑问,这一对宇宙本源的求索与困惑,实际上是对自身的生命价值的思索和探寻。古往今来,人类从未停止有关月亮的遐想,多少人曾经梦想登上月亮,而月亮始终高不可攀地用万里清辉普照尘世,伴随着无尽的时光。诗人将月亮比作明镜,夜出沧海,昼隐西山,昼夜交替,历史便在这交替中演变,表达了诗人对前进不息的时光的留恋和珍惜。在对神物和仙女寂寞命运的同情中,流露出诗人自己孤苦高洁的情怀。"今人不见古时月,今月曾经照古人"是在讲"前

Reflections on the Moon While Drinking

When did the moon first come on high?
I stop drinking to ask the sky.
The moon's beyond the reach of man;
It follows us where'er it can.
Like mirror bright o'er palace wall,
When clouds disperse, it's seen by all.
At night, it rises out of the sea;
At dawn, who knows where it can be?
Jade Hare* is not companion boon
For lonely Goddess of the Moon.

不见古人",而古月依旧,人生有限宇宙无穷,明月万古如一,而人类世代更替,同明月比起来,人类的有限生命真如沧海一粟。古人已流水一般逝去,今人的宿命也将如此,对着同一轮明月,古人今人关于人生和宇宙的意识得到统一。全诗意味深邃,诗人将明月与人生反复对照,在时间和空间的主观感受中,表达了对宇宙和人生哲理的深层思索。

* According to Chinese legend, the Jade Hare keeps company with the lonely Goddess of the Moon.

今人不见古时月,
今月曾经照古人。
古人今人若流水,
共看明月皆如此。
唯愿当歌对酒时,
月光长照金樽①里。

① 金樽：精美的酒具。

We see the ancient moon no more,
But it has shone on men of yore.
Like flowing stream, they passed away;
They saw the moon as we do today.
I only wish when I drink wine,
Moonlight dissolve in goblet mine.

白云歌送刘十六①归山

① 刘十六：李白友人。唐朝时，人们常用兄弟间排列次序来称呼人。

楚山②秦山③皆白云，
白云处处长随君。
长随君，
君入楚山里，
云亦随君渡湘水。
湘水上，
女萝衣④，
白云堪⑤卧君早归。

② 楚山：这里指今湖南地区，古时隶属于楚疆。

③ 秦山：这里指唐都长安，古时隶属于秦地。

④ 女萝衣：指的是屈原《九歌·山鬼》中的山中女神。

⑤ 堪：能，可以。

《白云歌送刘十六归山》是公元744年李白在长安为刘十六从终南山去楚山归隐而写的送别诗。诗写白云，也是写刘十六，因为白云是和隐士联系在一起的。白云自由不羁，高飞远走，清白无瑕，正是隐士品格的象征。刘十六归隐楚山湘水，湘水上的"女萝衣"就是屈原的"山鬼"准备送给隐士的。李白送别刘十六，其实是借他人酒杯浇自己胸中块垒，因为他对朝廷失望，也打算归山了。这首诗不少词语重叠，声韵流转，情怀摇漾，意境深远，是歌行中的上品。

Song of White Cloud
— Farewell Song to Liu the Recluse

From the mountains you come; to the mountains you go,

White clouds will follow you high and low, high and low.

When you come into Southern mountains high,

Following you, o'er Southern streams white clouds will fly.

O'er Southern water blue,

There's ivy cloak for you,

You should go back and lie on cloud as white clouds do.

秋日鲁郡尧祠亭上宴别杜补阙范侍御

我觉秋兴①逸,
谁云秋兴悲?
山将落日去,
水与晴空宜。
鲁酒白玉壶,
送行驻金羁②。
歇鞍憩古木,
解带挂横枝。
歌鼓川上亭③,
曲度神飙④吹。
云归碧海夕,
雁没青天时。
相失各万里,
茫然空尔思⑤。

① 秋兴:因秋起兴。

② 驻金羁:犹停马;金羁,金镶的马络头,这里指马。

③ 川上亭:水上的亭子,指尧祠亭。
④ 神飙:疾风。

⑤ 空尔思:徒然思念你们;尔,指李白好友杜补阙、范侍御二人。

　　这是一首送别诗。诗一开头因秋起兴,一扫逢秋悲寂寥的传统,抒发豪情逸致,展现了诗人旷达自适的宽广胸怀。在这样的逸兴中,秋日的景色,上下一体,浑然天成。眼前的景色被诗人赋予意识,有了个性和活力,视觉效果和宴会欢歌笑语的听觉效果融合在一起,营造出强烈的情感氛围。宴席的尾声,友人们依依惜别,从此天各一方,留下的是无尽的惆怅。

Farewell to Two Friends in Lu[*] on an Autumn Day

I feel that autumn's glad.

Who says that autumn's sad?

Hills bring down setting sun;

Water and sky seem one.

Drink wine from pot jade-white;

From golden horse alight.

Repose and set it free;

Hang belt upon old tree.

Chant by the stream aloud!

Songs soar into the cloud.

Back to blue sea clouds fly,

Wild geese lost in blue sky.

Like them we'll sever too,

In vain I'll long for you.

---

[*] Present-day Shandong Province.

鲁郡东石门①送杜二甫②

① 石门：山名，在今山东省曲阜市东北。

② 杜二甫：诗人杜甫，因排行第二，故称他为杜二甫。

醉别复几日，
登临遍池台。
何时石门路，
重有金樽开？
秋波落泗水③，
海色明徂徕④。
飞蓬⑤各自远，
且尽手中杯。

③ 泗水：水名，今在山东省东部。

④ 徂（cú）徕（lái）：山名，在今山东泰安市东南。

⑤ 飞蓬：一种植物，茎高尺余，叶如柳，花如球，因常随风飞扬旋转，名为飞蓬。

公元744年，李白与杜甫相识，两人一见如故。公元745年，李杜重逢，同游齐鲁。深秋，杜甫西去长安，李白再游江东，两人在鲁郡东石门分手，故有此篇。没有几天便要分别，不多的时间，用来痛饮，亭台楼阁都游览遍了，再也找不到留下的理由，不知何时能重聚，杜甫也说"何时一樽酒，重与细论文"，字里行间充满了两位大诗人惺惺相惜的不舍之情。徂徕泗水，秋色连波。在如诗如画的背景中，两位有着深厚情谊的友人似有千言万语，无尽的友谊化作一杯甘醇，结尾简洁干练，言有尽而意无穷。

Farewell to Du Fu at Stone Gate*

Before we part we've drunk for many days
And visit'd all the scenic spots and bays.
When at the Gate of Stone shall we meet and drain
Our brimming golden cups of wine again?
The autumn waves of River Si still flow;
The seaside mountains stand in morning glow.
You'll go away as thistle-down will fly,
So let us fill our cups and drink them dry.

* In present-day Shandong Province.

沙丘①城下寄杜甫

① 沙丘：指唐代兖州治城瑕丘。

我来竟何事？
高卧②沙丘城。
城边有古树，
日夕连③秋声。
鲁酒不可醉，
齐歌空复情。
思君若汶水，
浩荡寄南征。

② 高卧：高枕而卧，这里指闲居。

③ 连：连续不断。

这首诗大概是李白在鲁郡东石门送别杜甫后不久所作。开篇直言与杜甫分别后诗人生活的百无聊赖，不过终日高卧。所见不过城边的古树，在秋风中日夜发出瑟瑟之声。诗人通过萧瑟的秋风，诉说自己的苦闷孤寂，从而寄托自己的相思之意。没有知音，对从不离手的酒也失去了兴味，歌舞也徒有其声色。这两句的抒情大大加重了前句的情感，并为引出下文做足了铺衬。结尾诗人寄情于流水，河水奔腾不息，相思之意不绝，更好地抒发了诗人纯真而深沉的感情。

To Du Fu from Sand Hill Town[*]

Why have I come here after all
To live alone the whole day long?
There're but old trees by city wall,
From dawn till dusk but Autumn's song.
I can't be soothed by wine of Lu,
Nor moved by local melody.
Like River Wen I think of you,
Whose waves roll southward endlessly.

[*] In present-day Shandong Province.

戏赠杜甫

饭颗山①头逢杜甫,
头戴笠子日卓午②。
借问别来太瘦生③,
总为④从前作诗苦⑤。

① 饭颗山:山名。相传在长安一带。
② 日卓午:指正午太阳当顶。
③ 太瘦生:消瘦、瘦弱。生为语助词,唐时习语。
④ 总为:恐怕是因为。
⑤ 作诗苦:这里指杜甫一丝不苟的创作精神。

　　李白赠杜甫的诗现存三首:一首是《鲁郡东石门送杜二甫》,名句如"秋波落泗水,海色明徂徕",主要写二人的交游;一首是《沙丘城下寄杜甫》,名句如"思君若汶水,浩荡寄南征",主要写二人的交情,但都没有写出杜甫的特征。这首《戏赠杜甫》虽只短短四句,但却语言生动,使人如见烈日之下头戴竹笠形容消瘦的诗人,因为锤炼字句而搜索枯肠的形象,写出了诗人苦吟的精神,和杜甫《饮中八仙歌》描写的李白,形成了鲜明的对比。

Addressed Humorously to Du Fu

On top of Hill of Boiled Rice I met Du Fu,

Who in the noonday sun wore a hat of bamboo.

Pray, how could you have grown so thin since we did part?

Is it because the verse-composing wrung your heart?

梦游天姥①吟留别

① 天姥山:在浙江省绍兴市新昌县东面。传说登山的人能听到仙人天姥唱歌的声音,天姥山因此得名。

海客谈瀛洲②,
烟涛微茫信难求。
越人③语天姥,
云霞明灭或可睹。
天姥连天向天横,
势拔五岳掩赤城。
天台一万八千丈,
对此欲倒东南倾。
我欲因之梦吴越,
一夜飞渡镜湖月。

② 瀛洲:古代传说中的东海三座仙山之一(另两座叫蓬莱和方丈)。

③ 越人:指浙江一带的人。

《梦游天姥吟留别》是李白最重要的作品之一,作于公元746年他离开长安之后。诗人回首蓬莱宫殿,犹如梦游,就托天姥以寄意了。他因越人之语而幻想天姥,其实是因友人之荐而神往朝廷。诗中用夸张的手法写天姥山,因为它是朝廷的象征,入梦就象征入朝,"身登青云"。至于"半壁见海日,空中闻天鸡",就是召见金銮,侍诏翰林的景象了。他入朝以后发现朝中可惊可怖的现象,"熊咆龙吟""丘峦崩摧"。天姥山中的神仙洞府可能象征皇宫内院,自空而降的神仙就是贵族出游,场

Mount Skyland* Ascended in a Dream
— A Song of Farewell

Of fairy isles seafarers speak,

'Mid dimming mist and surging waves, so hard to seek;

Of Skyland Southerners are proud,

Perceivable through fleeting or dispersing cloud.

Mount Skyland threatens heaven, massed against the sky,

Surpassing the Five Peaks and dwarfing Mount Red Town.

Mount Heaven's Terrace, five hundred thousand feet high,

Nearby to the southeast, appears to crumble down.

Longing in dreams for Southern land, one night

I flew o'er Mirror Lake in moonlight.

面富丽堂皇,却又使人感到可怕,可见含有揭露之意。梦醒象征李白对朝廷幻想的破灭,所以才说:"世间行乐亦如此,古来万事东流水。"最后两句"安能摧眉折腰事权贵,使我不得开心颜!"说明这不是山水诗,不是游仙诗,不是留别诗,而是用比兴言志的手法,借梦游来抒发心中的愤懑,而诗人的形象和性格也在诗中显现出来了。

* Or Sky-Mother Mountains in present-day Zhejiang Province.

湖月照我影,
送我至剡溪①。
谢公②宿处今尚在,
渌③水荡漾清猿啼。
脚着谢公屐④,
身登青云梯⑤。
半壁见海日,
空中闻天鸡。
千岩万转路不定,
迷花倚石忽已暝。
熊咆龙吟殷岩泉,
栗深林兮惊层巅。

① 剡(shàn)溪:水名,在浙江省绍兴市嵊州市南面。
② 谢公:指南朝诗人谢灵运。
③ 渌(lù):清。
④ 谢公屐(jī):谢灵运穿的那种木屐。
⑤ 青云梯:指直上云霄的山路。

My shadow's followed by moonbeams

Until I reach Shimmering Streams,

Where Hermitage of Master Xie* can still be seen,

And clearly gibbons wail o'er rippling water green.

I put Xie's pegged boot

Each on one foot,

And scale the mountain ladder to blue cloud.

On eastern cliff I see

Sunrise at sea,

And in mid-air I hear sky-cock crow loud.

The footpath meanders 'mid a thousand crags in the vale,

I'm lured by rocks and flowers when the day turns pale.

Bears roar and dragons howl and thunders the cascade,

Deep forests quake and ridges tremble, they're afraid!

---

* Master Xie was a Jin-Dynasty poet who was fond of mountaineering and made himself special pegged boots for climbing.

云青青①兮欲雨,
水澹澹②兮生烟。
列缺③霹雳,
丘峦崩摧。
洞天石扉,
訇然④中开。
青冥浩荡不见底,
日月照耀金银台⑤。
霓为衣兮风为马,
云之君兮纷纷而来下。
虎鼓瑟兮鸾回车,
仙之人兮列如麻。
忽魂悸⑥以魄动,
恍惊起而长嗟。

① 青青:黑沉沉的。

② 澹澹:波浪起伏的样子。

③ 列缺:指闪电。

④ 訇(hōng)然:形容声音很大。

⑤ 金银台:金银铸成的宫阙,指神仙居住的地方。

⑥ 魂悸:心跳。

From dark, dark cloud comes rain;

On pale, pale waves mists plane.

Oh! Lightning flashes

And thunder rumbles,

With stunning crashes

Peak on peak crumbles.

The stone gate of a fairy cavern under

Suddenly breaks asunder.

So blue, so deep, so vast appears an endless sky,

Where sun and moon shine on gold and silver terraces high.

Clad in the rainbow, riding on the wind,

The Lords of Clouds descend in a procession long.

Their chariots drawn by phoenix disciplined,

And tigers playing for them a zither song,

Row upon row, like fields of hemp, immortals throng.

Suddenly my heart and soul stirred, I

Awake with a long, long sigh.

唯觉时之枕席，
失向来之烟霞。
世间行乐亦如此，
古来万事东流水。
别君去兮何时还？
且放白鹿青崖间，
须行即骑访名山。
安能摧眉折腰事权贵，
使我不得开心颜！

I find my head on pillow lie

And fair visions gone by.

Likewise all human joys will pass away

Just as east-flowing water of olden day.

I'll take my leave of you, not knowing for how long.

I'll tend a white deer among

The grassy slopes of the green hill

So that I may ride it to famous mountains at will.

How can I stoop and bow before the men in power

And so deny myself a happy hour?

登金陵凤凰台①

① 凤凰台：在金陵凤凰山上。

凤凰台上凤凰游，
凤去台空江自流。
吴宫②花草埋幽径，
晋代衣冠③成古丘。
三山④半落青天外，
二水⑤中分白鹭洲。
总为浮云能蔽日⑥，
长安⑦不见使人愁。

② 吴宫：指三国时孙吴于金陵建都筑宫。
③ 衣冠：原指衣服和礼帽，这里借指世族士绅、达官贵人、社会名流。
④ 三山：山名，在金陵西南长江边上，三峰并列，南北相连。
⑤ 二水：指秦淮河流经南京后，西入长江，被横截其间的白鹭洲分为二支。
⑥ 浮云蔽日：比喻谗臣当道，障蔽贤良。
⑦ 长安：这里指代朝廷和皇帝。

《登金陵凤凰台》是李白不多的七律中传诵最广的一首。凤凰形如孔雀，凤的出现表示祥瑞。现在凤去台空，引起了诗人怅然若失的感觉。第三、四句怀古：东吴和东晋都建都金陵，吴国的繁华宫苑只剩下了废墟小径，晋代的风流人物也进入了坟墓，令人顿生兴衰之感。第五、六句写景：三山半隐半现，若有若无，白鹭洲却把滔滔长江一分为二。这两句气势壮丽，对仗工整，是难得的佳句。最后两句抒怀：浮云蔽日暗示奸佞当道，皇帝受到蒙蔽，使自己报国无门。这样把典故、景物、感受交织在一起，抒发了诗人忧国忧时的怀抱，意旨深远。

On Phoenix Terrace at Jinling*

On Phoenix Terrace once phoenixes came to sing,
The birds are gone but still roll on the river's waves.
The ruined palace's buried 'neath the weeds in spring;
The ancient sages in caps and gowns all lie in graves.
The three-peak'd mountain is half lost in azure sky;
The two-fork'd stream by Egret Isle is kept apart.
As floating clouds can veil the bright sun from the eye,
Imperial Court now out of sight saddens my heart.

---

* Present-day Nanjing, capital of Jiangsu Province.

劳劳亭①

① 劳劳亭:在今江苏省南京市西南,为古时送别之所。

天下伤心处,
劳劳送客亭。
春风知②别苦,
不遣③柳条青。

② 知:理解。
③ 遣:让。

　　劳劳亭在南京,是古代送别的地方。李白不说天下伤心事是离别,只说天下伤心处是离亭,这样直中有曲,使读者会因地及事、由亭及人。因为送别时是早春,杨柳还没发青,不能折柳送别,于是诗人忽发奇想,说是春风深知离别之苦,不忍看到人折柳送别,所以故意不让杨柳发青了。这样把无情的杨柳说成有知有情,有伤别之心,这是化物为我,使春风成了诗人感情的化身,无怪乎古人说这两句诗"奇警无伦"了。

Pavilion Laolao*

There is no place that oftener breaks the heart
Than the Pavilion seeing people part.
The wind of early spring knows parting grieves,
It will not green the roadside willow leaves.†

* In present-day Nanjing.
† The Chinese had the custom of breaking off a green willow branch by the roadside and presenting it to the departing friend. The last line implies that the wind of early spring is unwilling to let friends sever.

丁都护歌①

① 丁督护歌：一名"阿督护"，乐府旧题。

云阳②上征③去，
两岸饶商贾④。
吴牛⑤喘月时，
拖船一何苦！
水浊不可饮，
壶浆半成土。
一唱都护歌，
心摧泪如雨。
万人凿磐石，
无由达江浒⑥。
君看石芒砀⑦，
掩泪悲千古！

② 云阳：今江苏丹阳。

③ 上征：指往北行舟。

④ 饶商贾（gǔ）：商人很多，指商业兴隆。贾，商人。

⑤ 吴牛：江淮间水牛。典故出自刘义庆《世说新语》："臣犹吴牛，见月而喘。"刘孝标注："今之水牛，唯生江淮间，故谓之吴牛也。南土多暑，而牛畏热，见月疑是日，所以见月则喘。"

⑥ 江浒（hǔ）：江边。浒，水边。

⑦ 石芒砀（dàng）：形容又多又大的石头。芒砀，大而多貌。

这是李白的《伏尔加河纤夫》。所用旧题本身就是凄切哀苦的。暑热时节，纤夫们拖船运石，穿着褴褛的衣衫，饮着浑浊的水，走过两岸富商云集繁华的河。不知何处传来《都护歌》，或许只是乐坊或茶楼酒肆的客人听腻了情歌艳曲，然而在纤夫们听来，不由得催人肺腑，泪如雨下。强烈的反差，深沉的笔触，表现了诗人对劳动人民的苦难命运的深切同情。

Song of the Tow-men

They tow a boat and upstream wade
Between two shores alive with trade.
Under the heat pants buffalo.
O think what pain it is to tow!
The water's muddy and can not
Be drunk: thick silt fills half the pot.
When tow-men sing their song's refrain,
With broken heart, tears fall like rain.
Ten thousand quarry-men would groan
To haul to riverside rough stone.
If rocky mountains could have ears,
Would they not melt into sad tears?

苏台①览古

① 苏台：即姑苏台，其旧址在今江苏省苏州市西南姑苏山上。

旧苑荒台杨柳新，
菱歌②清唱③不胜春。
只今惟有西江月，
曾照吴王宫里人④。

② 菱歌：东南水乡老百姓采菱时唱的民歌。
③ 清唱：形容歌声婉转清亮。
④ 吴王宫里人：指吴王夫差宫廷里的嫔妃。

公元 742 年，李白游姑苏台时作此诗。昔日的雕梁画栋，昔日的舞榭歌台，如今都已经荒废。莎翁的十四行诗中有一句最脍炙人口："荒芜的歌场，曾是鸟儿啁啾的地方"，与此诗可谓异曲同工，极为传神地传达繁华尽逝后的萧瑟与荒凉。见证过这里繁花似锦的，如今只剩一轮明月，依旧照着断壁残垣。此诗既是作者对时过境迁、世事难料的感慨，也是对历史的喟叹。

The Ruin of the Gusu Palace*

Deserted garden, crumbling terrace, willows green,
Sweet notes of *Lotus Song* cannot revive old spring.
All are gone but the moon o'er West River that's seen
The ladies fair who won the favor of the king.

---

* The Gusu Palace in present-day Suzhou is where the king of Wu with his beautiful Xi Shi held perpetual revelries till the king of Yue annihilated him in the fifth century B.C.

越中①览古

① 越中：指会稽，春秋时代越国曾建都于此。故址在今浙江省绍兴市。

越王勾践破吴②归，
义士还家尽锦衣。
宫女如花满春殿③，
只今惟有鹧鸪④飞。

② 勾践破吴：此处指越王勾践卧薪尝胆终破吴国的故事。

③ 春殿：宫殿。

④ 鹧鸪：鸟名。形似母鸡，头如鹑，胸有白圆点如珍珠，背毛有紫赤浪纹，叫声凄厉。

唐代的越州在今天的浙江绍兴，是越王勾践建都的地方。公元前472年，越王勾践灭了吴王夫差，胜利归来，战士个个脱下盔甲，穿上锦衣，宫中美女个个如花似玉。这首诗和《苏台览古》不同，《苏台览古》两联都是兴衰对比，这首却是前三句写景，最后一句才写鹧鸪飞的荒凉景象。前面写乐景越有力，后面写哀景就一句顶三句了。

The Ruin of the Capital of Yue

The king of Yue* returned, having destroyed the foe,
His loyal men came home, with silken dress aglow,
His palace thronged with flower-like ladies fair;
Now we see but a frock of partridges flying there.

---

* The king of Yue destroyed the kingdom of Wu in the 5th century B.C.

越 女 词

（五首其一）

长干^①吴^②儿女^③，
眉目艳星月。
屐上足如霜，
不着鸦头袜^④。

① 长干：地名，在今浙江北部。
② 吴：吴地，在今长江下游江苏南部。
③ 儿女：此指女儿。
④ 鸦头袜：叉头袜。

《越女词》共五首，是李白漫游吴越时的作品，描写吴越民间女子的容貌和服饰，显示出江南水乡的旖旎风光。诗的风格清新活泼，有浓厚的民歌色彩。这首诗描写吴家儿女美丽的容貌和活泼的姿态。词句不事雕琢，风格质朴，具有典型的太白诗风。

Songs of the Southern Lass

(I)

The Southern lass is fair and bright,
Her eyes and brows shame moon and stars.
Her feet in sandals are frost-white,
The crow-head shoes would look like scars.

越女词

（五首其三）

耶溪①采莲女，
见客棹歌②回。
笑入荷花去，
佯羞不出来。

① 耶溪：即若耶溪，在今浙江省绍兴市南。
② 棹歌：划船时所唱之歌。

这首诗写的是天真娇羞的采莲姑娘的形象。采莲女水中采莲，忽闻有客乘舟而来，赶紧掉转方向，躲进密密麻麻的荷丛之后，仿佛是因为怕羞而不敢见客一般。诗的题材和语言受南朝民歌影响，清新自然，返璞归真，令人神驰遐想。

Songs of the Southern Lass

(III)

A maiden gathers lotus in the creek,

Singing, she turns round, seeing passers-by.

Smiling, she hides 'mid lotus blooms her cheek

And won't appear again: she seems so shy.

越女词

（五首其五）

镜湖①水如月，

耶溪女如雪。

新妆荡新波，

光景②两奇绝。

① 镜湖：又称鉴湖、庆湖，在今浙江省绍兴市会稽山北麓，周围三百里若耶溪北流入于镜湖。

② 景（yǐng）：同"影"。

镜湖在今天的浙江绍兴，若耶溪相传是西施浣纱的地方。溪水流入湖中，明净如月光的湖水，照着粉妆素裹的少女，波光人影相互辉映，景使人更美，人使景更丽。本诗是李白借美景写美人的佳作。

Songs of the Southern Lass

(V)

The waves of Mirror Lake look like moonbeams;
The maiden's dress like snow on waterside.
The rippling dress vies with the rippling stream,
We know not which by which is beautified.

渌水曲[1]

[1] 渌(lù)水曲：古乐府曲名；渌水：绿水，清澈的水。

渌水明秋月，
南湖[2]采白蘋[3]。
荷花娇欲语，
愁杀[4]荡舟人。

[2] 南湖：即洞庭湖。

[3] 白蘋：一种水生植物，是多年生浅水草本，根茎在泥中，叶子浮在水面之上。

[4] 愁杀："愁煞"，愁得不堪忍受的意思；杀：用在动词后，表示极度。

这首小诗写的是思念远人带来的愁绪。开局从一个明媚的秋日写起，粼粼波光中少女荡舟采蘋。见荷花粉红娇嫩，含羞欲语，恰如少女的年纪清纯，只是荷花娇嫩尚有人观赏，而自己正当盛年却无人陪伴，莫名的愁绪涌来。也有人认为诗人是在用一贯的夸张手法，写自己荡舟湖上，见荷花如少女含羞欲语，让采蘋的姑娘们非常不满，犹言荷花的美。

Song of Green Water

O'er water green the autumn moon shines bright,
On Southern Lake they gather lilies white.
The lotus-blooms so lovely as to speak
Outshine the bashful oarswomen's fair cheek.

闻王昌龄左迁龙标遥有此寄

杨花①落尽子规②啼,
闻道龙标③过五溪④。
我寄愁心与明月,
随风直到夜郎⑤西。

① 杨花:柳絮。
② 子规:杜鹃鸟,又称布谷鸟,相传其啼声哀婉凄切,甚至啼血。
③ 龙标:诗中指王昌龄,古人常用官职或任官之地的州县名来称呼一个人。
④ 五溪:是武溪、巫溪、酉溪、沅溪、辰溪的总称,在今湖南省西部。
⑤ 夜郎:唐代夜郎县,位于今湖南省怀化市沅陵县。

　　王昌龄因不拘细节,被贬黜到五溪之西的龙标(今天的湖南省怀化市沅陵县)。从他的诗句"一片冰心在玉壶"来看,对他的处分是太重的,因此李白写了这首诗寄给他。暮春时节,百花凋残,杨花落尽,加上子规悲啼"不如归去",这时李白听到王昌龄贬官的消息,见景生情,分外凄凉。但是两人一东一西,同看到的只有春风明月,于是李白就把明月人格化,托它把自己的相思之情带去千里之外,梦乡之西了。这是一首融情景、叙事于一炉的名作。

To Wang Changling Banished to the West

All willow-down has fallen and sad cuckoos cry
To hear you banished southwestward beyond Five Streams.
I would confide my sorrow to the moon on high
For it will follow you west of the Land of Dreams.*

* Present-day Guizhou Province.

战 城 南

去年战,
桑干①源;
今年战,
葱河②道。
洗兵③条支④海上波,
放马天山雪中草。
万里长征战,
三军尽衰老。
匈奴以杀戮为耕作,
古来惟见白骨黄沙田。
秦家筑城备胡处,
汉家还有烽火燃。
烽火燃不息,
征战无已时。
野战格斗死,
败马号鸣向天悲。

① 桑干:桑干河,为今永定河之上游,于今河北省西北部和山西省北部。
② 葱河:葱河即葱岭河。今有南北两河。南名叶尔羌河,北名喀什噶尔河。
③ 洗兵:洗去战斗后兵器上的污秽。
④ 条支:汉西域古国名。在今伊拉克底格里斯河、幼发拉底河之间。此泛指西域。

Fighting South of the Town

Last year we fought

At River's source;

This year we fight

Along its course.

We've washed our swords in Parthian seas off bloody stains,

And grazed our horses on the grass in mountain's snow.

For miles and miles we made campaigns

Till weak and old our warriors grow.

The Tartars live on killing as on ploughing land,

Bleach'd bones of olden times are buried in the sand.

Under the Qin* against the foe Great Wall was raised;

Under the Han† the beacon fires still blazed.

See beacon fires on the frontier!

Till warriors fight from year to year.

In wilderness the fighters die,

Riderless horses neigh toward the sky;

---

* The Qin Dynasty (221–207 B.C.).

† The Han Dynasty (206 B.C.–220 A.D.).

乌鸢①啄人肠，

衔飞上挂枯树枝。

士卒涂草莽，

将军空尔为。

乃知兵者是凶器，

圣人不得已而用之。

① 鸢(yuān)：老鹰，属于鹰科的一种小型的鹰，常啄食腐烂肉。

    天宝年间（742—756），唐玄宗轻启战端，给百姓带来深重的灾难。有人说李白的写作风格是开门见山，在此诗中的确是这样，开篇即以战始，直接抨击了当权者穷兵黩武，好杀伐之功，以致连年征战。左思《魏都赋》描写曹操讨灭群雄、威震寰宇的气势时说："洗兵海岛，刷马江洲。"李白借用其意，说明军队征讨太远。不敢想象，等这些远征万里的青壮年两鬓斑白回到家中时，家中还有几人。而比起那永远没有机会回来的人，即使"归来头白还戍边"，他们也还算幸运的。匈奴人不务耕作，专事征战掠夺。秦时防备匈奴的长城，汉代仍然烽火常燃。长久的军事斗争，使大量的青壮年白白牺牲，残尸曝烈日，流血涂野草，换来的只是"将军空尔为"，揭露了为官者为博取功名不惜"一将功成万骨枯"的残酷本性。诗以《六韬》"圣人号兵为凶器，不得已而用之"做结尾，来总结历史经验，劝当道者不要滥用武功。

Crows pecking human entrails flee

And hang them on a withered tree.

The blood of soldiers smears the grass.

Without them what could generals do?

War is a fearful thing, alas!

For rulers wise, 'twould be the last means resorted to.

听蜀僧濬①弹琴

① 蜀僧濬：即蜀地名濬的僧人。

蜀僧抱绿绮②，
西下峨眉峰。
为我一挥手，
如听万壑松③。
客心洗流水④，
余响⑤入霜钟⑥。
不觉碧山暮，
秋云暗几重？

② 绿绮：琴名。

③ 万壑松：指万壑松声。此处以万壑松声比喻琴声。

④ 流水：语意双关，既是对僧濬琴声的实指，又暗用了伯牙善弹的典故。

⑤ 余响：指琴的余音。

⑥ 霜钟：指钟声。

《听蜀僧濬弹琴》是李白写音乐的一首五言律诗。李白是四川人，对故乡一往情深。他对峨眉山来的和尚情有独钟，一听他挥手弹起名贵的绿绮琴来，就像听到万山中松涛起伏一样。松风琴韵像流水般洗净了他的凡心俗念，余音袅袅，不绝如缕。琴声和霜降时的寺庙晚钟融合在一起，听来大有高山流水遇知音之感。不知不觉，琴声更融入了碧山秋云之中，似乎天地都在和琴声共鸣了。这是一首表现弹者和听者心灵交流的好诗。

On Hearing a Monk from Shu* Playing His Lute

A monk from Shu his green lute brings,

Coming down the west peak of Mount Brow.

He sweeps his fingers o'er its strings,

I hear the wind through pine-trees sough.

A running stream washes my heart,

With evening bells its echo's loud.

I do not feel the sun depart

From mountains green and autumn cloud.

---

* Present-day Sichuan Province.

寄东鲁二稚子

吴地①桑叶绿,
吴蚕已三眠②。
我家寄东鲁③,
谁种龟阴田④?
春事⑤已不及,
江行复茫然。
南风吹归心,
飞堕酒楼前。
楼东一株桃,
枝叶拂青烟⑥。
此树我所种,
别来向三年⑦。
桃今与楼齐,
我行尚未旋。
娇女字平阳,
折花倚桃边。

① 吴地:今江苏一带,春秋时属吴国。

② 三眠:蚕蜕皮时,不食不动,其状如眠。蚕历经三眠,方能吐丝结茧。

③ 东鲁:今山东一带,春秋时属鲁国。

④ 龟阴田:此处指李白在山东的田地。

⑤ 春事:春日耕种之事。

⑥ 拂青烟:拂动的青烟,形容枝繁叶茂状。

⑦ 向三年:快到三年了。

Written for My Two Children in East Lu[*]

Mulberry leaves in Southern land are green,

The silkworms thrice in sleep must have been.

In Eastern Lu my family stay still.

Who'd help to sow our fields north of Lu Hill?

It's now too late to do farmwork of spring.

What then am I to do while travelling?

The southern wind is blowing without stop,

My heart flies back to my old familiar wine shop.

East of the shop there's a peach tree I've missed,

Its branches must be waving in bluish mist.

It is the tree I plant'd three years ago,

If it has grown to reach the roof, I don't know.

I have not been at home for three long years.

I can imagine my daughter appears

Beside the tree and plucks a flower pink.

---

[*] Present-day Shandong Province.

折花不见我，

泪下如流泉。

小儿名伯禽，

与姐亦齐肩。

双行桃树下，

抚背复谁怜？

念此失次第①，

肝肠日忧煎。

裂素②写远意，

因之汶阳川。

① 失次第：心绪不定，七上八下。

② 裂素：指准备书写工具之意；素，绢素，古代作书画的白绢。

    这是李白写给自己两个孩子的家书。公元748至750年，李白游金陵，思念他寄居东鲁的家人，故有此篇。诗人看到吴地春景，即景生情，想到家中春天正是农事繁忙之际，而自己浪迹江湖，一事无成，龟山北面的田园正不知该找谁代耕。念及此，不禁心生焦虑。春天的农事已来不及了，而今后仍漂泊不定，不知归期。每每思家，家里熟悉的一切都会浮现眼前：那小酒楼，那棵亲手种下的桃树。作者对家中的一切倾注

Without seeing me, she must have, I think,
Shed copious tears. My younger son has grown
Up to his sister's shoulders. 'Neath full-blown.
Peach tree they stand side by side. But who's there
To pat them on the back? I feel, whene'er
I think of this, so painful that I write
And send to them this poem on silk white.

了深厚的感情，为下文引出对儿女的思念营造了浓厚的氛围。诗人写对儿女的思念，先不言自己相思之情，而从儿女思父的角度入手，一片思念之情，自然流泻。最后从想象当中回归现实，将相思寄于汶水。毋庸置疑，诗人情景并茂的奇丽想象，是这首诗神韵飞动、感人至深的重要原因。

秦王扫六合

秦王扫六合,
虎视何雄哉!
挥剑决浮云,
诸侯尽西来。
雄图发英断,
大略驾群才。
收兵铸①金人,
函谷正东开。
铭功会稽②岭,
骋望琅琊台。
刑徒七十万,
起土骊山隈③。
尚采不死药,
茫然使心哀。
连弩射海鱼,
长鲸正崔嵬④。

① 铸:把金属熔化后倒在模子里制成器物。

② 会稽:中国古代郡名,位于长江下游江南一带。

③ 隈:形容山水弯曲的地方。

④ 崔嵬:形容物体高大的样子。

The Emperor of Qin

The Emperor had swept the world of his foes,

Looking around like a tiger he rose.

He broke the floating clouds while wielding swords,

Westward to pay their homage came all lords.

He made great plans and formed decisions wise,

In front of him all heroes dwarfed in size.

He melted weapons into statues of brass,

And opened to the East the frontier pass.

He built a monument on Eastern Hill,

And rode to Southern Tower to gaze his fill.

He worked seven hundred thousand slaves

To build in deep mountain recess his graves.

He sought elixir of immortality,

These contradictory deeds puzzle me.

He bent his bow to shoot the monster whale

Sweeping the sea with its enormous tail.

额鼻象五岳,

扬波喷云雷。

鬐鬣^①蔽青天,

何由睹蓬莱?

徐市载秦女,

楼船几时回?

但见三泉下,

金棺葬寒灰!

① 鬐(qí)鬣(liè):鱼脊和鱼颔上的羽状部分。

　　李白对秦始皇的评价,是毁誉参半的,也是比较客观的。首先他肯定了秦始皇的历史功绩,对秦始皇的正面颂扬也很有气势,但这显然不是大诗人真正想表达的。疲弊天下,严刑峻法,期不死,筑高陵,求仙药,猎长鲸,最后却"但见三泉下,金棺葬寒灰",这才是诗人的本意,深刻地揭露了秦始皇自私、贪婪、空虚、恐惧的内心世界。李白站在超越时间、超越客观历史的角度,用大部分的篇幅批判秦始皇,实属借古讽今:唐玄宗也和秦始皇一样,早年励精图治,开创了唐朝的极盛时期——开元盛世,后来又变得骄奢淫逸,怠慢朝政,最后迷信方士妄求长生。李白此诗,历史结合夸张想象,叙事结合抒情,批判现实主义结合浪漫主义,挥洒自如,跌宕生姿,是不可多得的佳作。

Its head and nose erect'd like mountains proud,

And water spout'd like thunder and like cloud.

Its dorsal fin might cover azure sky.

Could seamen find the Fairy Islands* high?

The alchemist with maidens went to sea.

When could their galleys come back? We but see

Buried in underworld, the ashes cold

Of Emperor of Qin in coffin made of gold!

---

* The Emperor of Qin (reigned 246–210 B.C.) sent an alchemist to sea to seek for the elixir of immortality in the Fairy Islands. The alchemist reported that a monster was barring the seaway and the Emperor shot dead a giant whale.

登高丘而望远海

登高丘,

望远海。

六鳌①骨已霜,

三山流安在?

扶桑②半摧折,

白日沉光彩。

银台金阙③如梦中,

秦皇汉武空相待。

精卫费木石,

鼋鼍④无所凭。

① 六鳌:传说渤海的东面是无边无际的大海,上面浮着岱舆、员峤、方壶、瀛洲、蓬莱五座神山,山上长有长生不老药;鳌,传说中海里的大鳖。

② 扶桑:神话中树木名。传说太阳每天在咸池沐浴后,升高到扶桑树梢的时候,刚好天微明。

③ 银台金阙:黄金白银建成的亭台宫阙,指神仙居住的地方。

④ 鼋(yuán)鼍(tuó):鼋,大鳖;鼍,鼍龙,俗称猪婆龙,鳄鱼的一种。传说周穆王征越国,在九江架鼋鼍为桥渡江。

此诗的主体部分几乎每一句都藏着一个典故。这并不是怀古之章,主旨与《秦王扫六合》一样,是用典故做隐喻,借古讽今,语言比《秦王扫六合》更加深刻露骨。诗人由登高望远点题,联想到传说神话中的仙人神物并不存在于现实世界。李白是喜爱于深山之中访仙问道的,这是因为他不被现实世界所理解,不被世俗所接收,所以他只能寻找超脱世俗之路,寻求精神上的寄托。所以他更加明白根本没有什么神仙,妄图通过求仙问道以求长生更是愚不可及。用秦皇汉武的典故类比,是对此类皇帝的讽刺和批判,是对当朝皇帝的暗示。

Mounting a Height* and Viewing the Sea

Mounting a height,

I gaze afar.

Six Giant Turtles' bones emerge on sea, frost-white,

I do not see where the Three Fairy Mountains are.†

The Tree Divine half broken,

The sun's great splendours wane.

Celestial palace is a dream unwoken

Emperors sought in vain.

The sea could not be filled with stones,

Nor could the gap by Turtles' bones.

---

* Mount Tiantai in present-day Zhejiang Province.

† According to Chinese legend, elixir could be found in the Fairy Mountains borne by Giant Turtles on the sea, but six Turtles were killed and Fairy Mountains floated off we know not where.

君不见,
骊山茂陵尽灰灭,
牧羊之子①来攀登!
盗贼劫宝玉,
精灵②竟何能?
穷兵黩武今如此,
鼎湖飞龙安可乘?

① 牧羊之子:《汉书·刘向传》记载,有个牧童在骊山牧羊,有一只羊进入山洞中,牧童用火照明,到洞里去寻羊,以致引起一场大火,把秦始皇的外棺烧掉了。

② 精灵:指秦皇、汉武的神灵。

Have we not seen imperial tombs in ruins lie,

Which shepherds set on fire?

The bandits came to rob your jewels of value high.

What could you do, imperial lier?

Such is the end you warmongers obtained.

Could immortality be ever gained?

北 风 行

烛龙①栖寒门，
光耀犹旦开。
日月照之何不及此②？
惟有北风号怒天上来。
燕山雪花大如席，
片片吹落轩辕台。
幽州思妇十二月，
停歌罢笑双蛾摧③。
倚门望行人，
念君长城④苦寒良可哀。

① 烛龙：中国古代神话传说中的龙。传说此龙住在极北的寒门，终日不见太阳，睁眼为昼，闭眼为夜。

② 此：指幽州，在今北京市南郊。

③ 双蛾摧：双眉紧锁，形容悲伤、愁闷的样子。双蛾：女子的双眉。

④ 长城：此处泛指北方前线。

《北风行》是乐府调名，内容多写北风雨雪、行人不归的伤感之情。李白于公元752年秋游幽州时，目睹当地百姓饱受战火的痛苦而作此诗。诗的开头通过怪诞离奇的神话，展现一个幽冷严寒的北方世界。以此为基础，作者又进一步描写足以显示北方冬季特征的景象："日月照之何不及此？惟有北风号怒天上来。燕山雪花大如席，片片吹落轩辕台。"落笔大气，意境雄浑壮阔，故成千古名句。接下来诗人塑造了一个忧心忡忡、愁肠百结的思妇形象，塞北苦寒，征人的困境不言自明，更引起对远在长城的丈夫的担心。"提剑救边"刻画了丈夫为国慷慨从戎的英武形象。如果说离家日久，蛛网纵横已使人黯然神伤，箭尚在，人空守则使人不忍。思妇含恨焚箭这一举动将全篇的情感酝酿到最高点，在结尾强烈地爆发出来。

The North Wind

The candle-holding Dragon curls o'er Polar Gate,*
Only at dawn his flickering light will radiate.
Nor sun nor moon will shine there far and nigh,
Only the howling northern wind blows down from the sky.
The snowflakes from north mountains, big as pillows white,
Fall flake on flake upon Yellow Emperor's Height.†
The twelfth moon sees the wife in lonely bower sit,
She will nor sing nor smile, with eyebrows tightly knit.
She leans against the door and looks at passers-by,
Thinking of her husband who with cold might shiver
Beyond the Great wall and sigh.

---

* According to Chinese myth, the North Pole was illuminated by the candle held by a dragon whose eyes would make day when opened and night when closed.
† The Yellow Emperor was believed to be an ancestor of the Chinese people and inventor of south-seeking compass.

别时提剑救边去,
遗此虎文金鞞靫①。
中有一双白羽箭,
蜘蛛结网生尘埃。
箭空在,
人今战死不复回。
不忍见此物,
焚之已成灰。
黄河捧土尚可塞,
北风雨雪恨难裁!

① 鞞(bǐng)靫(chá):绘有虎纹图案的箭袋。

When he started, his sword in hand,

To save the borderland.

He left her two white-feathered arrows in a golden quiver.

The pair of arrows 'mid cobwebs and dust remain.

Her lord who fell in battle won't come back again.

How could she bear to see the tiger-striped quiver?

She tries to burn it into ashes.

Building a dam, we may stop the flow of Yellow River.

How could the northern wind assuage her grief that gashes!

横 江 词

（六首其一）

人道横江①好，
侬道②横江恶。
一风三日③吹倒山，
白浪高于瓦官阁。

① 横江：横江浦，是古代的长江渡口。
② 道：一作"言"。
③ 三日：一作"一月"。

横江，即横江浦，在今安徽省马鞍山市和县东南，位于长江西北岸，与东南岸的采石矶相对，形势险要。前两句颇有民歌风味，"侬"为吴人自称，"人道""我道"一抑一扬，为引出下文做好转折。后两句作者用一贯的夸张手法，极力状写横江"阴风怒号，浊浪排空"。这首诗主要是写横江的地势险峻，气候多变，诗人以想象丰富奇伟的笔触，创造出雄伟壮阔的境界。

The Crosswise River

(I)

They say the Crosswise River good;

I say the Crosswise River rude.

If winds should blow three days,

E'en hills would be blown down,

And waves rise higher than the Temple* in the town.

* The Temple was 240 feet in height, to the southwest of present-day Nanjing.

山中问答

问余^①何意栖碧山,
笑而不答心自闲。
桃花流水窅然^②去,
别有天地非人间^③。

① 余:我,诗人自指。

② 窅(yǎo)然:幽深遥远的样子。

③ 非人间:这里指诗人的隐居生活。

公元 753 年,李白曾在湖北省安陆市的碧山隐居读书,这首七言绝句可能是那时写的。第一句问得突兀,第二句以不答为答,显得轻松愉快、悠闲自得。第三句再写自然景象,表明心如桃花流水,悠然远去,可见诗人热爱自由。第四句"别有天地非人间",可见诗人热爱自然超过尘世。后来南唐李煜的名句"流水落花春去也,天上人间",可能得益于李白。但是白诗淡远,煜词沉痛,真是一个天上,一个人间了。

A Dialogue in the Mountain

I dwell among green hills and someone asks me why,
My mind carefree, I smile and give him no reply.
Peach blossoms fallen on running water pass by,
This is an earthly paradise beneath the sky.

自 遣

对酒①不觉暝,
落花盈②我衣。
醉起步溪月,
鸟还人亦稀。

① 对酒:与朋友对饮。
② 盈:洒满。

如果说《山中问答》是写山居悠闲的乐趣,这首《自遣》就是山居生活的写照。第一句"对酒不觉暝",说的是整日读书饮酒,不知不觉天就晚了,真是神仙生活,因为神仙不就是壶中天地大,书中日月长吗?第二句"落花盈我衣",似乎是接着《山中问答》第三句"桃花流水窅然去"而言的,说桃花不但落在流水上,而且落满我一身,这不是成了桃花仙吗?第三句"醉起步溪月",说不但落花有意于流水,诗人和明月也是一样流连忘返。最后一句"鸟还人亦稀",是说鸟归人归,我独不归,这就是诗人与众不同的地方。因为"真"是自然规律的需要,"善"是社会规律的需要,两者都是客观需要,只有爱"美"是人的主观需要,表达了人的自由,表达了诗人高于万物的需求。

Solitude

I'm drunk with wine
And with moonshine,
With flowers fallen o'er the ground
And o'er me the blue-gowned.
Sobered, I stroll along the stream
Whose ripples gleam,
I see not a bird
And hear not a word.

独坐敬亭山①

① 敬亭山：在今安徽省宣城市北。

众鸟高飞尽，
孤云独去闲②。
相看两不厌③，
只有敬亭山。

② 闲：形容云彩飘来飘去，悠闲自在的样子。
③ 厌：满足。

《独坐敬亭山》是李白公元753年秋游宣城时写的一首小诗。第一句"众鸟高飞尽"先写众鸟之"动"，然后一个"尽"字却是静态；第二句"孤云独去闲"也是先写孤云之动，然后一个"闲"字表示静态。前两句都是以"动"衬"静"，以物喻人，"孤"和"闲"写的是云，其实也象征诗人的孤独和悠闲。后两句"相看两不厌，只有敬亭山"却是静态，写诗人对山有情，山对诗人也有情，这就把山人格化了。山有情可以反衬出权贵对诗人无情；诗人和山互相有情则是达到情景交融、"天人合一"的境界了。

Sitting Alone in Face of Peak Jingting*

All birds have flown away, so high;
A lonely cloud drifts on, so free.
We are not tired, the Peak and I,
Nor I of him, nor he of me.

---

* North of Xuancheng, in present-day Anhui Province.

宣州^①谢朓楼饯别^②校书叔云^③

① 宣州：今安徽省宣城市一带。
② 饯别：以酒食送行。
③ 叔云：李白的叔叔李云。

弃我去者，
昨日之日不可留；
乱我心者，
今日之日多烦忧。
长风^④万里送秋雁，

④ 长风：远风，大风。

对此可以酣高楼。
蓬莱文章建安骨，
中间小谢又清发。

公元753年，李白和路过宣城的叔父李云在南齐太守谢朓修建的高楼上饮酒，写下了这首饯别诗。第一句的"昨日"，可能指唐玄宗"开元盛世"；第二句的"烦忧"，可能暗示杨国忠和安禄山等当权，使诗人报国无门，只能登楼饮酒。叔侄二人目送长风万里，秋雁南飞，诗人却不能乘风破浪，为国出力，不禁感慨系之，于是二人谈起蓬莱文章和建安风骨来。蓬莱指秘书省，而李云是秘书省校书，他的文章有《吊古战场文》；建安风骨则指曹植等的文风；小谢就是谢朓，其诗文清新秀发，李白非常欣赏。诗人虽然心怀豪情壮志，梦想飞天揽月，但是抽刀不能断水，只得借酒浇愁，不料却又愁上加愁了。人生在世，不如意的事太多，只好学孔子"道不行，乘桴浮于海"。

Farewell to Uncle Yun, the Imperial Librarian, at Xie Tiao's Pavilion in Xuanzhou*

What left me yesterday

Can be retained no more;

What troubles me today

Are the times for which I feel sore.

In autumn wind for miles and miles the wild geese fly.

Let's drink, in face of this, in the pavilion high.

Your writing's forcible like ancient poets while

Mine is in Junior Xie's clear and spirited style.

---

* Xie Tiao or Junior Xie (464–499) was a poet of the Jin Dynasty, who built a pavilion or the North Tower in Xuanzhou (present-day Xuancheng in Anhui Province).

俱怀逸兴壮思飞,
欲上青天揽明月。
抽刀断水水更流,
举杯消愁愁更愁。
人生在世不称意,
明朝散发①弄扁舟②。

① 散发(fà):去冠披发,指隐居不仕。古人习惯束发,而散发表示闲适自在。
② 弄扁(piān)舟:乘小舟归隐江湖。

Both of us have an ideal high:

We would reach the moon in the sky.

Cut running water with a sword, 'twill faster flow;

Drink wine to drown your sorrow, it will heavier grow.

If we despair of all human affairs,

Let us roam in a boat with loosened hairs!

秋登宣城谢朓北楼

江城①如画里,
山晚望晴空。
两水②夹明镜③,
双桥④落彩虹⑤。
人烟寒橘柚,
秋色老梧桐。
谁念北楼上,
临风怀谢公?

① 江城:水边的城,这里指宣城。

② 两水:指宛溪与句溪。

③ 明镜:指拱桥桥洞和与其倒影在水中合成的圆形,像明亮的镜子一样。

④ 双桥:指凤凰桥与济川桥。

⑤ 彩虹:指水中的桥影。

　　本诗作于公元753年秋天。李白在长安为权贵所排挤,弃官而去后,一直过着漂泊不定的生活。当秋风摇落的时节,诗人内心的抑郁和感伤是可以想象的。如诗如画的宣城,一个晴朗的秋天的傍晚,诗人独自登上了谢公楼。一片晴空之中,河水如镜,长桥如虹。橘柚在袅袅炊烟的映衬之下越发苍寒,梧桐在秋色笼罩下也显得越发苍凉。苍凉旷达的意境显现出来,更写出了诗人内心理想无法实现的惆怅、落寞。最后点明怀念谢朓,抒发了对先贤的追慕之情,同时抒发自己理想难以实现的感慨。

On Ascending the North Tower One Autumn Day

The scroll-like River-town's steeped in twilight,
In view of mountains 'neath a lucid sky.
Two rivers, mingling, form a mirror bright;
Two bridges like rainbows fallen from on high.
The cottage smoke has chilled the orange flower;
The autumn hue has oldened parasol trees.
Who ever dreamed I'd come up Northern Tower
To meditate on Xie in western breeze?

送友人

青山横北郭①,
白水②绕东城。
此地一为别,
孤蓬③万里征。
浮云游子意,
落日故人情。
挥手自兹去,
萧萧④班马⑤鸣。

① 郭:古代在城外修筑的一种外墙。

② 白水:清澈的水。

③ 孤蓬:此处诗人指远行的朋友;蓬:古书上说的一种植物,干枯后根株断开,遇风飞旋。此处比喻远行的朋友。

④ 萧萧:马的呻吟嘶叫声。

⑤ 班马:离群的马,这里指载人远离的马。

　　这是一首充满诗情画意的送别诗。第一联"青山"对"白水",静态的"横"对动态的"绕","北郭"又对"东城",对仗工丽,别开生面。第二联说友人就要像蓬草一样漂泊万里了,离情依依。第三联"浮云"象征友人行踪不定,"落日"徐徐西下,暗示诗人不忍离别之心;青山绿水,白云红日,色彩绚丽,富有画意。第四联"挥手"又以动态入画,"萧萧"马鸣之声入耳,更是有声有色,余音久久不绝。这首五言律诗有景有情,情景交融,扣人心弦。

Farewell to a Friend

Green mountains bar the northern sky;
White water girds the eastern town.
Here is the place to say goodbye,
You'll drift out, lonely thistledown.
Like floating cloud you'll float away;
With parting day I'll part from you.
We wave and you start on your way,
Your horse still neighs: "Adieu! Adieu!"

秋浦①歌

（十七首其十四）

① 秋浦：县名，唐时先属宣州，后属池州，在今安徽省池州市贵池县西。秋浦因流经县城之西的秋浦河得名。

炉火②照天地，
红星乱紫烟。
赧郎③明月夜，
歌曲动寒川。

② 炉火：指炼铜之炉火。

③ 赧（nǎn）郎：红脸汉。此指炼铜工人；赧：原指因羞愧而脸红，此处形容脸被炉火所映红。

李白从宣城到秋浦来游山玩水，写了17首《秋浦歌》，这里选的第14首。秋浦是唐代银和铜的产地之一，这是一首正面描写和歌颂冶炼工人的诗歌，因在古代诗歌中非常少见而极为可贵。秋浦寂静的月色中，冶炼厂的炉火燃起来了，飞溅的火星闪烁在被冲天的火光照成紫色的烟当中。炉火映红了人们的脸，照亮了周围的夜。工人的歌声震撼着寂静的大地，也震荡着寒冷的水面。在诗人如神的笔下，光、热、声、色，明与暗、冷与热、动与静交相辉映，共同交织成一幅瑰丽壮观的画面，生动地再现了热火朝天的劳动场景，绘声绘色地塑造了古代冶炼劳动者的形象。

Songs of Autumn Pool

(XIV)

The furnace fire makes bright the earth and sky,
Into the purple smoke red sparks wild fly.
The blacksmiths' faces flush in moonlit night,
Their songs would fill the river cold with fright.

秋 浦 歌
（十七首其十五）

白发三千丈，

缘愁似个①长。　　　　　　　① 个：如此，这般。

不知明镜里，

何处得秋霜②？　　　　　　　② 秋霜：形容人的头发花白，宛如秋霜。

　　这一首是以夸张闻名的典型。第一句"白发三千丈"劈空而来，使人如见丈二金刚，摸不着头脑。第二句"缘愁似个长"点明，原来是忧愁使白发变得这样长的。那忧愁该有多么深重啊！诗人揽镜自照，大吃一惊，这哪里是满头白发，分明是饱经风霜的衰草嘛！这秋霜又是从哪里得来的呢？全诗戛然而止，发人深思，使人想起诗人饱经风霜的一生。

Songs of Autumn Pool

(XV)

My whitened hair would make a long, long cord,

As long as I am often bored.

I know not how the mirror bright

Reflects a head with hoarfrost white.

赠汪伦

李白乘舟将欲行,
忽闻岸上踏歌①声。
桃花潭②水深千尺③,
不及汪伦送我情。

① 踏歌:唐代民间流行的一种手拉手、边走边唱的歌舞形式。
② 桃花潭:在今安徽省宣城市泾县西南一百里。
③ 深千尺:诗人用深千尺的潭水比喻汪伦与他的友情,运用了夸张的手法。

《赠汪伦》是李白赠别诗中传诵最广的一首。据说汪伦写信给李白说:"先生好游乎? 此地有十里桃花;先生好酒乎? 此地有万家酒店。"李白欣然而来,汪伦却笑着说:"十里桃花是十里外的桃花潭,万家酒店是姓万的人开的酒店。"李白听了大笑。游完桃花潭后,李白正要离去,忽然汪伦同村人手拉着手,脚步踏着拍子来送行了。于是李白又用夸张手法,写下了这首像说话一般自然的好诗。

To Wang Lun Who Comes to Bid Me Farewell

I, Li Bai sit aboard a ship about to go,

When suddenly on shore footsteps and songs o'erflow.

The Lake of Peach Blossom is a thousand fathoms deep,

But not so deep as the friendship Wang Lun and I keep.

哭晁卿衡[①]

[①] 晁卿衡：即晁衡，日本人，原名阿倍仲麻吕（又作安倍仲麻吕）。公元717年（日本灵龟二年，唐开元五年），来中国求学，后改名为晁衡。

日本晁卿辞帝都，
征帆一片绕蓬壶[②]。
明月[③]不归沉碧海[④]，
白云愁色满苍梧[⑤]。

[②] 蓬壶：指蓬莱、方壶，都是神话传说中东方大海上的仙山。此处喻为晁衡在东海中航行。
[③] 明月：形容品德高洁才华出众之士。
[④] 沉碧海：此处指溺死海中。
[⑤] 苍梧：九嶷山，此指传说中东北海中的郁州山（郁洲山）。

此诗是公元754年，李白听闻晁衡（日本人阿倍仲麻吕）归国时遇暴风失事的消息后所作。诗人以友人的身份，听闻晁卿如同明月沉大海一去不返，顿觉连苍梧山都被愁云笼罩。此诗虽因误传噩耗而作，但悲痛之情是真实而且深挚的，表现了两人超越国界的深厚友谊。

Elegy on Abe Nakamaro*

My Japanese friend Abe left the imperial shore,

His single sail turned round for the three Fairy Isles.

The moon has sunk in the sea to return no more,

The land's o'erspread with gloomy clouds for miles and miles.

---

* Abe Nakamaro came to China (referred to as the imperial shore in this poem) in 717 at the age of 20 and did not return to Japan (referred to as the three Fairy Isles) till the winter of 753. It was rumoured that he (referred to as the moon) was drowned in the sea and Li Bai wrote this poem.

永王东巡歌

（十一首其二）

三川①北虏②乱如麻，
四海南奔似永嘉。
但用东山③谢安石，
为君谈笑静胡沙。

① 三川：指河、洛、伊三川，于今河南省洛阳市。
② 北虏：指安禄山叛军。
③ 东山：谢安隐居处。

《永王东巡歌》作于公元757年，李白随永王李璘水帅东下浔阳之时，现存11首。洛阳沦陷后一片混乱，士人争相躲避江东。诗人以谢安自居，自谓在国家大难当头时，希望像谢安一样从容镇静地破敌除患，希望永王重用自己。诗人在诗中表现的是爱国志士的热诚，对遭受战火的百姓的同情。他想做谢安那样的儒将，从容应敌，决胜千里，虽然是不现实的，甚至是幼稚的，却成就了他豪迈的浪漫主义风格。

Song of Eastern Expedition of Prince Yong
(II)

Three River Valleys overrun by Northern foes,

People within four seas flee to the Southern land.

If Master Xie* again from Eastern Mountain rose,

He'd quell with ease the rebels as he'd sprinkle sand.

---

* Xie An fought against heavy odds and won victory in 382. Here the poet alluded to himself.

与史郎中①钦听黄鹤楼上吹笛

① 郎中：官名，为朝廷各部所属的高级部员。

一为迁客②去长沙③，
西望长安不见家。
黄鹤楼中吹玉笛，
江城④五月落梅花。

② 迁客：被贬谪之人。

③ 去长沙：此处指贾谊因受权臣谗毁，贬为长沙王太傅之事。

④ 江城：指江夏（今湖北省武汉市武昌区），因在长江、汉水滨，故称江城。

李白于公元758年流放夜郎经过武昌时，游黄鹤楼，写下此诗。诗人先引贾谊为同调，用贾谊的不幸来比喻自身的遭遇，对自己的无辜受害表示忧愤。长安远在万里之外，那里已经没有家了，去路茫茫，不知前方有什么在等待着，诗人不免感到惆怅，这时响起的笛声使他感到格外凄凉，仿佛五月的江城落满了梅花。诗人巧借笛声来渲染愁情。时值初夏，诗人听见《梅花落》犹如置身漫天飘落的梅花之中，不觉寒气凛凛，正是诗人心情冷落的写照，传神地表达了怀念帝都之情和"望"而"不见"的愁苦。

On Hearing the Flute in Yellow Crane Tower

Since I was banished to the riverside town,

Looking westward, I've found no house I'd call my own.

Hearing in Yellow Crane Tower the flute's sad tune,

I seem to see mume blossoms fall in the fifth moon.*

---

* The mume blossoms blow in winter or spring, not in summer (the fifth moon). Hearing the flute, the poet became so sad as to take summer for winter.

早发①白帝城

① 发:启程。

朝辞白帝彩云间②,
千里江陵③一日还。
两岸猿声啼不住,
轻舟已过万重山④。

② 彩云间:因白帝城在白帝山上,地势高耸,从山下江中仰望,仿佛耸入云间。

③ 江陵:今湖北荆州市。

④ 万重山:层层叠叠的山;万重:形容数目之多。

公元758年,李白因为支持永王而被流放夜郎,船在长江逆流而上,几乎走了一年。他到白帝城时,忽然遇赦返回江陵,喜出望外,写了这首快诗:一是船快,二是心情愉快。"朝辞白帝"是和白帝城告别,也是和过去告别,心情舒畅;"彩云间"既写城高,又写心情好,看云也美,白帝城成了"仙居"。"千里江陵一日还"用空间之远和时间之短对比,显得船行"神速"。猿鹤本是"仙侣",原为沉船哀啼,李白遇赦听来,却似乎是在和过去告别。最后一句的"轻舟"暗示卸下心头重担,"万重山"一过,前途就是"天路"般的康庄大道了。"仙居""神速""仙侣""天路",使这首七言绝句成了仙气洋溢的"谪仙诗"。

Leaving the White Emperor Town* for Jiangling†

Leaving at dawn the White Emperor crowned with cloud,
I've sailed a thousand *li* through Canyons in a day.
With monkeys' sad adieux the riverbanks are loud;
My skiff has left ten thousand mountains far away.

* In present-day Sichuan Province.
† In present-day Hubei Province.

与夏十二①登岳阳楼

① 夏十二：李白的朋友，因在家中排行十二，故称夏十二。

楼观岳阳②尽，
川迥洞庭开。
雁引愁心去，
山衔好月来。
云间连下榻，
天上接行杯。
醉后凉风起，
吹人舞袖回③。

② 岳阳：今湖南省岳阳市，以在天岳山之南，故名。

③ 回：回荡，摆动。

公元 759 年，李白到江陵后，南游岳阳，同他的朋友夏十二（排行十二）登上了岳阳楼。凭栏远望，天岳山南无边景色尽收眼底，河水流向洞庭湖，浩荡开阔，汪洋无际。秋雁高飞，带走了诗人忧愁之心；月出山口，仿佛是高山吐出了明月。在岳阳楼上饮酒，潇洒自如！全诗没写一个高字，只从周围景物的浩渺、开阔、高耸落笔，无处不显得楼高，同时写出了诗人的超脱豁达、豪情逸志。

Ascending the Tower of Yueyang* with Xia the Twelfth

On scenes so vast the Tower feasts our eye;

The river stretches into the Lake of South.†

Taking away our sorrow, wild geese fly;

Green mountains throw the moon up from their mouth.

Make of white cloud a comfortable bed,

And pass around wine cups in azure skies.

Drunken, let cooling breezes blow and spread

Our dancing sleeves which flap like butterflies.

---

* In Hunan Province.

† The Dongting Lake.

陪族叔刑部侍郎晔及中书贾舍人至游洞庭

(五首其二)

南湖①秋水夜无烟,
耐可②乘流直上天?
且③就洞庭赊月色,
将船买酒白云边。

① 南湖:指洞庭湖。因在长江之南,故称南湖。

② 耐可:哪可,怎么能够。

③ 且:姑且。

此诗为公元759年李白与李晔、贾至同游洞庭时所作。全组共五首,这一首最为出色。清澈的夜里,湖光山色,粼粼水波似乎直通天上银河。丰富浪漫的想象,夸张的表述,好一幅洞庭秋夜图。月色如许,这样的境界下,最易使人忘怀。暂且就着湖里的月色倒影,当作是泛舟天上,像神仙一样在云边沽酒。诗人即景发兴,酣畅淋漓,好似一幅浓墨泼就的山水画。

On Lake Dongting*

(II)

Vaporless is the Southern Lake on autumn night.
Could we be borne to Heaven by the rising tide?
If we could borrow from Lake Dongting the moonlight
To guide us skyward, we'd drink with clouds by our side.

* In Hunan Province.

江上吟

木兰①之枻②沙棠舟,
玉箫金管坐两头。
美酒樽③中置千斛④,
载妓随波任去留。
仙人有待乘黄鹤,
海客⑤无心随白鸥。
屈平⑥词赋悬日月,
楚王台榭空山丘。
兴酣⑦落笔摇五岳,
诗成笑傲凌沧洲。
功名富贵若长在,
汉水⑧亦应西北流。

① 木兰:即辛夷,香木名。
② 枻(yì):同"楫",舟旁划水的工具,即船桨。
③ 樽:盛酒的器具。
④ 千斛:形容船中置酒极多;斛:古时十斗为一斛。
⑤ 海客:海边的人。
⑥ 屈平:指屈原,名平,战国末期楚国大诗人。
⑦ 兴酣:诗兴浓烈。
⑧ 汉水:发源于陕西省汉中市宁强县,东南流经湖北省襄阳市,至汉口汇入长江。汉水向西北倒流。此处比喻不可能的事情。

此诗为公元743年李白游江夏时所作。这首诗以江上的遨游起兴,表现了诗人对庸俗、局促的现实的蔑弃,和对自由、美好的生活理想的追求。诗人以屈原自比,抒发胸臆,末尾带着嘲弄的意味,说明富贵功名都是尘俗之物不可能长久。诗人追求的是一种自由的、超脱了世俗功利的生活。

Song on the River*

In a ship of spice-wood with unsinkable oars,
Musicians at both ends, we drift along the shores.
We have sweet wine with singing girls to drink our fill,
And so the waves may carry us where'er they will.
Immortals could not fly without their yellow crane;
Unselfish men might follow white gulls to the main.
The verse of Qu Ping† shines as bright as sun and moon,
While palaces of Chu vanish like dreams at noon.
Seeing my pen in verve, even the mountains shake;
Hearing my laughter proud, the seaside hermits wake.
If worldly fame and wealth were things to last forever,
Then northwestward would turn the eastward-flowing river.

---

* In Hubei Province.
† Qu Yuan (340–270 B.C.) was a loyal minister and great poet in the state of Chu.

夜宿①山寺

①宿：住，过夜。

危楼②高百尺，
手可摘星辰。
不敢高声语，
恐惊天上人。

②危楼：高楼，这里指山顶的寺庙。

如果说《与夏十二登岳阳楼》是写景抒情之作，那《夜宿山寺》就是一首想象丰富的浪漫主义小诗。前者不说楼高，只写周边景物，却用烘云托月法衬出楼高；后者直说"危楼高百尺"，而用想象"手可摘星辰"的夸张手法来充实叙述。这样虚中有实、实中有虚的写法，使人虚实不分，模模糊糊，更会觉得寺高。接着"不敢高声语"又是实写，"恐惊天上人"却是虚假的想象。前两句写所见所感，后两句写所听所闻，这样虚虚实实，有声有色，就使人如见"山外青山楼外楼"了。

The Summit Temple*

Hundred feet high the Summit Temple stands,
Where I could pluck the stars with my own hands.
At dead of night I dare not speak aloud
For fear of waking dwellers in the cloud.

* In present-day Hubei Province.

庐山谣寄卢侍御虚舟

我本楚狂人[1]，
凤歌笑孔丘。
手持绿玉杖[2]，
朝别黄鹤楼。
五岳寻仙不辞远，
一生好入名山游。
庐山秀出南斗傍，
屏风九叠云锦张，
影落明湖青黛光。
金阙[3]前开二峰长，
银河[4]倒挂三石梁。

[1] 楚狂人：春秋时楚人陆通因不满楚昭王的政治，佯狂不仕，故称"楚狂"。此处李白以陆通自比，表现对政治的不满，要像楚狂那样游览名山过隐居的生活。

[2] 绿玉杖：镶有绿玉的杖，传说为仙人所用。

[3] 金阙指黄金的门楼，这里借指庐山的石门。阙：皇宫门外的左右望楼。

[4] 银河：指瀑布。

公元760年，李白60岁的时候和卢虚舟同游庐山。他遇赦归来后，看破红尘，想要修仙学道，写这首诗给卢虚舟，劝他不要做官。诗人把自己比作楚国狂人，唱《凤歌》劝孔子仕途知返，退隐深山。接着，他就描写庐山在南斗星座之下，好像张开了云锦做的九叠屏风，倒影映在鄱阳湖里，闪烁着墨绿色的反光。石门好像仙人打开的金阙，两旁双峰耸立，中间有瀑布流出，犹如银河倒挂在三道石梁上，那就是三叠泉。遥遥相对的是香炉峰瀑布。这些重峦叠嶂，仿佛要飞上青天。庐山翠影和朝阳彩霞相映成趣，吴地天空辽阔，连鸟也飞不到边。登上庐山观望

Song of Mount Lu*

— To Censor Lu Xuzhou

I'm just a freak come from the South,
With frank advice e'er in my mouth.
Holding at dawn a green-jade cane,
I leave the Tower of Yellow Crane.
Of the long trips to Sacred Mountains I make light,
All my life I have loved to visit famous height.
Lu Mountains tower high beside the wain stars bright
Like a nine-panelled screen embroidered with clouds white.
Their shadows fall into the lake like emerald;
Two peaks stand face to face above the Gate of Gold.
A waterfall is hanging down from Three Stone Beams,

天地之间,只见茫茫长江一去不还;万里黄云飘浮,天色瞬息变幻;长江九条支流已经涌起雪山般的波涛,令人触目惊心。因此,诗人就对着石镜来清除尘心,看见谢灵运的足迹已被苍苔埋没,幸亏自己早已服了九转金丹,没有留恋尘世的感情;心如琴弦,修炼已有初步成效,可以遥望手拿莲花的仙人去天宫了。诗人已和"汗漫"仙约好同游太空,他问卢虚舟愿不愿同游。这首诗反映了李白不满现实、逃避现实的出世思想。

* In present-day Jiangxi Province.

香炉瀑布遥相望,
回崖沓嶂①凌苍苍。
翠影红霞映朝日,
鸟飞不到吴天长。
登高壮观天地间,
大江茫茫去不还。
黄云②万里动风色,
白波九道流雪山。
好为庐山谣,
兴因庐山发。
闲窥石镜清我心,
谢公行处苍苔没。
早服还丹③无世情,
琴心三叠④道初成。
遥见仙人彩云里,
手把芙蓉朝玉京。
先期汗漫九垓⑤上,
愿接卢敖游太清⑥。

① 回崖沓嶂:曲折的山崖,重叠的山峰。

② 黄云:昏暗的云色。

③ 还丹:道家炼丹,将丹烧成水银,积久又还成丹,故谓"还丹"。

④ 琴心三叠:道家修炼术语,指一种心神宁静的境界。

⑤ 九垓:九天之外。

⑥ 太清:天空。

Cascades of Censer Peak like upended silver streams.
Cliff on cliff, ridge on ridge lead to the azure skies,
Their green shapes kindled by flaming clouds at sunrise
Barring the boundless Heaven's vault where no bird flies.
I climb to view the sky o'erhead and earth below,
The ne'er-returning waves of the River onward go.
In yellow clouds outspread for miles I see wind blow,
Nine foaming tributaries splash like mountain snow.
Of Mountain Lu I love to sing,
Of my poetry it is the spring.
I gaze at the Stone Mirror, my heart purified,
I seek the poet Xie's path which green mosses hide.
Elixir swallowed, I care not what people say;
The zither played thrice, I begin to know the Way.
I see from afar immortals in the cloudy land,
They come to celestial city, lotus-bloom in hand.
I'll go before you somewhere beyond the ninth sphere
And wait for you to wander in the Zenith Clear.

豫 章 行

胡风①吹代马②,
北拥鲁阳关③。
吴兵④照海⑤雪,
西讨何时还?
半渡上辽津,
黄云惨无颜。
老母与子别,
呼天野草间。
白马绕旌旗,
悲鸣相追攀。
白杨秋月苦,
早落豫章山。

① 胡风:北风。

② 代马:代地(今山西省东北与河北省张家口市蔚县一带)所产的良马。此处指胡马。

③ 鲁阳关:战国时称鲁关,汉称鲁阳,在今河南省平顶山市鲁山县西南。

④ 吴兵:吴越之地的征调之兵士,泛指江南之兵。

⑤ 海:指鄱阳湖。

《豫章行》为乐府《清调曲》调名,古辞写豫章山上白杨变为洛阳宫中栋梁,述其与根株分离之苦。李白借用旧题,描写行军作战的悲壮情景。诗人是矛盾的,朝廷的征兵,造成了多少亲人的生离死别和家庭的破碎,给人民带来多大的苦难,诗人看在眼里。而征兵对朝廷来说实属无奈之举,为了维持国家的和平,必须做出牺牲。所以诗人更多的流露出来的是同情和祝愿,这正是诗人忧国忧民的写照。

Song of Yuzhang*

The horses neigh to hear the north wind blow,
The rebels† occupy the Northern Pass.
The Southern armour bright as lake-side snow,
When will our men be back from war? Alas!
Half of them are aboard, ready to part,
E'en yellow clouds look gloomy and turn pale.
Old mothers see their sons off, sad at heart,
Crawling amid wild grass, they weep and wail.
Around the flags turn steeds which parting grieves,
They chase each other, foaming at the mouth.
'Neath autumn moon the poplars shed their leaves
Early which cover mountains of the South.

* Present-day Nanchang, capital of Jiangxi Province.
† An Lushan who rebelled in 755.

本为休明人①,
斩虏素不闲。
岂惜战斗死,
为君扫凶顽②。
精感石没羽,
岂云惮险艰?
楼船若鲸飞,
波荡落星湾。
此曲不可奏,
三军发成斑。

① 休明人:太平盛世时期的人。休明:形容生活美好清闲。

② 凶顽:凶暴愚顽之人。

I am a man living in time of peace,

Not used to fighting or exchanging blows.

But I am not afraid to fight without cease,

And sweep away our formidable foes.

Our concentrated efforts could break stone

And enemy however hard they are.

Our galleons swift like whales which might have flown

O'er waves which surge in the Bay of Falling Star.*

This isn't a tune for army-men to play:

On hearing it, their hair would soon turn grey!

---

* Present-day Poyang Lake of Jiangxi Province.

哭宣城①善酿纪叟

① 宣城:在今安徽省东南。

纪叟黄泉里,
还应酿老春②。
夜台③无李白,
沽酒与何人?

② 老春:唐人称酒多有"春"字,此处指纪叟所酿酒名。
③ 夜台:坟墓。亦借指阴间。

  李白在宣城为悼念一位善于酿酒的纪师傅,写下了这首纸短情长的悼亡诗。句句写的都是虚拟中的纪叟死后之事,这是一个特殊的抒情角度。诗人说纪叟在黄泉下,还应该在酿老春酒,这就等于说明了纪叟生前是酿酒的。说"夜台无李白,沽酒与何人",等于说明李白是纪叟生前的老主顾。这样写就是以简驭繁的。第二个特殊的角度,诗中又幻想纪叟还活着,依旧在黄泉下酿酒。纪叟怎么能不死呢?因为诗人不相信他死了,也不忍心让他死去。这里写的不是客观的事实,而是主观的感情。这样表达出来的悲痛和友情,比一般的友情要深得多。第三个特殊的角度,诗人不说自己如何怀念纪叟,反说纪叟在怀念自己。这样从对方的角度写,等于把两个人的感情加在一个人身上,感情的分量和抒情的效果都增加了一倍。李白诗的本色,正是用天然的语言,表示最深挚的感情。这首小诗可以说是他最后的代表作,因为不久之后,他就离开了人世。译诗中写虚拟之事,没有用虚拟语态,而是用了陈述语气,仿佛纪叟真没有死,这样表示的友情,比用虚拟式又更深了一层。

Elegy on Master Brewer Ji of Xuancheng*

For thirsty souls are you still brewing
Good wine of Old Spring, Master Ji?
In underworld are you not ruing
To lose a connoisseur like me?

---

* In present-day Anhui Province.

宣城见杜鹃花

蜀国①曾闻子规鸟②,
宣城还见杜鹃花③。
一叫一回肠一断,
三春三月忆三巴④。

① 蜀国:指四川。
② 子规鸟:又名杜鹃,因鸣声凄厉,动人乡思,故俗称断肠鸟,传说是古蜀王杜宇死后幻化而成。
③ 杜鹃花:即映山红,因每年春末盛开,恰逢杜鹃鸟啼之时,故名杜鹃花。
④ 三巴:巴郡、巴东、巴西三郡,即指蜀国,今四川。

写这首诗的时候,李白已是迟暮之年。流放途中遇赦的他,流落江南,晚景凄凉。看见杜鹃花开,想起蜀中这时节,杜鹃也开始啼叫了,可是这杜鹃啼血是最听不得的呀,诗人的思乡情肠被触动了,况且当年他仗剑去国,辞亲远游,正待施展雄才大略,何等潇洒,如今功业未成,岁月蹉跎,缠绵病榻,不知能否再见故乡,满心的悲戚和浓浓的乡愁不觉涌上心头。

Azalea Blooms Viewed in Xuancheng

I've heard home-going cuckoos sing in Western Towers[*],

And here and now I see the blooming cuckoo flowers[†],

I turn away: my heart will break to hear them sing,

For they remind me of my homeland in late spring.

[*] In present-day Sichuan Province, homeland of the poet.
[†] Chinese name for azalea flowers which bloom when cuckoos cry "Go home!" and according to Chinese legend, shed bloody tears.

临终歌

大鹏飞兮振八裔①,
中天②摧兮力不济。
余风③激兮万世,
游扶桑④兮挂⑤左袂⑥。
后人得之传此,
仲尼亡兮谁为出涕⑦?

① 八裔(yì):八方荒原之地。
② 中天:半空。
③ 余风:遗风。
④ 扶桑:古代神话传说中的大树,生在太阳升起的地方。古代把太阳作为君主的象征。此处暗喻到了皇帝身边。
⑤ 挂:喻腐朽势力阻挠。
⑥ 左袂:左边衣袖。
⑦ 仲尼亡兮谁为出涕:指孔子泣麟的典故。传说麒麟是一种祥瑞的异兽。鲁哀公十四年(前481年),鲁国猎获一只麒麟,孔子认为麒麟出非其时,而被捕获,非常难受。

　　这是李白为自己撰写的墓志铭。李白终其一生都在为实现自己的理想和远大抱负而奋斗,他视自己为大鹏的化身,大鹏永远是振翅翱翔的形象。但这只大鹏再也飞不动了,他觉得自己这样一只大鹏已经飞到不能再飞的时候了,他便长歌当哭,为大鹏唱一支悲壮的《临终歌》。李白在诗中回顾自己一生的时候,流露的是对人生无比眷念和未能才尽其用的深沉惋惜。或许,在他生命的尽头,一只振翅高翔的大鹏永远定格在了他的心中。

On Death-Bed

When flies the roc, he shakes the world.
In mid-air his weakened wings are furled.
The wind he's raised still stirs the sea,
He hangs his left wing on sun-side tree.
Posterity mine, hear, O, hear!
Confucius dead, who'll shed a tear?

图书在版编目（CIP）数据

许渊冲译李白诗选：汉文，英文 /（唐）李白著；
许渊冲编译 . -- 北京：中译出版社，2021.1（2022.7 重印）
（许渊冲英译作品）
ISBN 978-7-5001-6450-0

I. ①许… II. ①李… ②许… III. ①唐诗－诗集－汉、英 IV. ①I222.742

中国版本图书馆 CIP 数据核字（2020）第 240378 号

出版发行	中译出版社
地　　址	北京市西城区新街口外大街28号普天德胜大厦主楼4层
电　　话	(010)68359719
邮　　编	100088
电子邮箱	book@ctph.com.cn
网　　址	http://www.ctph.com.cn
出 版 人	乔卫兵
总 策 划	刘永淳
责任编辑	刘香玲　张　旭
文字编辑	王秋璎　张莞嘉　赵浠彤
营销编辑	毕竞方
赏　　析	李　旻
封面制作	刘　哲
内文制作	黄　浩　北京竹页文化传媒有限公司
印　　刷	天津新华印务有限公司
经　　销	新华书店
规　　格	840mm×1092mm　1/32
印　　张	8.75
字　　数	200千
版　　次	2021年1月第1版
印　　次	2022年7月第3次

ISBN 978-7-5001-6450-0　定价：46.00元

版权所有　侵权必究

中 译 出 版 社